To Cara
Happy [signature]

A PLAN UNRAVELLED

One bad decision can derail any well-thought-out plan

A NOVEL

LIA SPENCER

Elephant House Press
www.elephanthousegroup.com
Edinburgh, SA, Australia
elephanthousepress@gmail.com

© Lia Spencer 2019

ISBN: 9780648490319

All rights reserved. Except for private study, research, criticism or reviews, as permitted under the Copyright Act, no part of this book may be reproduced, stored in a retrieval system, or transmitted in any form or by any means without prior written permission. Enquiries should be made to the publisher.

Cataloguing-in-Publications entry is available from the National Library of Australia http:/catalogue.nla.gov.au

First edition published 2019

Original Cover Image by Alissa Dinallo

DEDICATION

For Isla and Louis,
I hope that the fear of failing never stops you
from chasing your dreams.
I love you to the moon and back.

ONE

Ten minutes.

That's all I had between make-up and filming. I usually took this time, be it ten minutes, fifteen or sometimes only thirty seconds, to grab some water or rehearse my lines in my caravan. I shouldn't have strayed from routine.

Ten minutes. That's all it took for me to destroy every bit of success I'd achieved in the past fifteen years.

I'd only been eight when I'd written out Ruby's Master Plan:

Move to New York.

Get an acting gig.

Make money.

I'd ticked them all off by the age of eighteen.

What wasn't on my young, ambitious list was being found facedown in a shift dress and knee-high boots, with specs of vomit in my glorious back-combed wig. Classy. In fact, neither was moving back to Australia nor falling in love with an ex-con.

My plan not only backfired, it exploded in a furious force of flames and burned to a crisp, leaving all my ambitions in a pile of ashes.

If my eight-year-old self had known what was to come, I would have been distraught. More distraught than the day her hamster got his leg stuck in its wheel and died helplessly and alone of an unfortunate blood rush to the head.

That had been the most devastating day of my short life, but Mum bought me a goldfish a few days later and Hammy the hamster became a distant memory.

If only our problems could be as easily fixed as they were back then. My publicist, Michelle, assured me they could be. She insisted that I go into hiding for three months while she executed her damage control plan.

Three months, she said. That's all it would take for her to clean up the mess I'd created. That's all it would take for the smoke to subside and for me to get back on my feet and start over.

TWO

February
Melbourne, Australia

'Are you ready, Ruby?'

That's a loaded question.

'You'll be fine; I'm only a phone call away.' The shrink peered at me over her thick-rimmed glasses, the kind I wore when I played a sexy secretary in a romantic comedy that went straight to video. Though I'm sure she'd said those lines several times before, they weren't scripted. And as much as I wished this was all an act, it was my new reality.

She signed a form on her desk and stuck it in my file. 'Now you can head back to your room and pack your bags. You're going home.'

Home. Right. She wasn't talking about New York. She was talking about Rockford. The place in the middle of nowhere, where Starbucks was unheard of and a chilli dog was only found in a kennel, mid-winter. After nearly fifteen years, I wasn't ready to go back. I would have preferred to hide out in a private villa in

Greece or a quaint log cabin in the Canadian Rockies, but my bank account was drained and I'd run out of options. I dreaded moving back to Rockford, but it was more appealing than the alternative. I couldn't stomach the thought of asking Dad for money, then getting pummelled with questions of where my thousands had gone.

Sure, I had a larger salary than the average person my age, or any age for that matter, but a penthouse apartment in Manhattan, trendy clothes and A-list parties didn't come cheap. And when trying to make a name for myself, I'd had to dig deep to keep up.

Okay, fine. I'd been careless with my spending. In hindsight, I should have let Michelle handle my funds when she'd suggested it years ago, but she already had a million hats on her head, and to be honest, I'd been too proud to be put on a budget. I'd never had one before. Surely, if dad did ask how I could be so reckless, I could tell him that he was to blame.

Michelle came into my life as an agent, but because she is a control freak, added personal assistant and publicist to her credentials. I didn't know how she managed to do all three and not suffer a major breakdown like I had, but she was magical at what she did and she never skipped a beat. She found pride in calming commotions and sorting through chaos. She was loyal but professional. If she knew what I'd been doing behind the scenes, she never let on.

If I'd known everything that happened behind the scenes, maybe I wouldn't have ended up in the movie industry. But there'd been no stopping me. I'd wanted so desperately to become an actress ever since my mother took me to see a live musical when I was a little girl.

It was a matinee performance, so she didn't show any compassion as I yawned and carelessly flicked through the program. Instead, she leaned in close, her nose brushing my ear, and whispered, 'Musicals are the trifecta of the art world, Ruby.'

Most kids wouldn't understand, but having watched Dad place many bets over the years, it made perfect sense to me.

I sat with my legs crossed, blew bubbles with my chewy and rolled my eyes as everyone took their seats around us. But when the lights went out, and the show began, the stage wrapped a firm grip around me. I was hostage to the detailed set. Captivated by the small black space as it transformed into a cityscape with sky-high buildings, streetlights and snow. Blowing snow. Snow that looked so real I felt like I was stuck in the dead of winter, with a freezing sting on my bare skin and an overwhelming urge to open my mouth to catch the flakes on my waiting tongue. I had never experienced temperatures low enough for snow to fall, but in that moment, I'd understood what it was like to live in it, to feel it, to see my breath when I spoke, to have numb toes when I stood.

Just as I began to fall in love with winter, the snow melted and sparrows took flight. Limbs of large trees swaggered in the wind and mounds of sand rested at the roots. Strands of hair blew across children's faces as they swung from swings and teetered on seesaws with a laughter that echoed throughout the hall.

The changing sets coincided with musical performances that raised the hair on my arms. There were beautiful costumes with lace and pearls and sparkling diamonds. I was so fixated on the beautiful actors – the way they moved with grace, the way they sang with passion – that when the show was over, I wanted more.

Mum insisted we leave with the crowd, but I pulled on her sleeve and dug in my heels until she agreed to let me hover by the backstage door in a desperate effort to meet the cast. After about an hour of waiting, I finally met the people who were responsible for sparking a fiery passion that, until then, had lain dormant in my veins.

If they had told me the truth that day, the lows instead of the highs, then maybe I wouldn't have pleaded with my parents to enrol me in acting classes, maybe I wouldn't have spent sleepless nights dreaming about the red carpet and acceptance speeches, and maybe I wouldn't have boarded a plane when I was seventeen, in pursuit of my dreams. And maybe I wouldn't have hit rock bottom fifteen years later.

A nurse stood at the end of my bed. Stern-faced, she beckoned with one finger.

I folded up the one photo I'd kept in my room and tucked it into the top pocket of my suitcase. The picture was dark and faded and the corners were tattered. It was of my brother Jimmy and me – him about nine and me, twelve. We were dressed as angels for a school play. Jimmy had developed a love for guitar and strummed a few lines in that Christmas play that year. He was going to be a rock star one day, he told me. He would play alongside the likes of Eric Clapton, The Police or U2. Even through the worn photo, Jimmy's young, fresh face radiated and his eyes glistened. But, crippled by high-expectations and fears of not measuring up, he never pursued his dream. In fact, he never left home. Years of living off our parent's handouts eventually battered his motivation, and his new addictions weathered his pale, narrow face.

I flung my leather jacket over my arm and quietly groaned as I struggled to pick up my suitcase. Nearly three weeks without exercise and I had already lost my strength and found my bingo wings – a term Michelle used to refer to the jiggly skin under the arms – the sight horrified her.

The nurse hurried ahead, leading me towards reception. Except for a large whiteboard on the wall, the halls were spotless and smelled sterile, like a hospital should. But it also felt like death – cold and lonely.

Goosebumps crept up my arm at the sight of Mum standing at the nurse's station. The last time I'd spoken to her, she was a sobbing mess. She blamed herself. She shouldn't have. But she'd been there from the beginning, guiding me through auditions, flying with me to New York, helping me get set up and supporting me through my career. So, she was consumed with guilt when Michelle called to tell her what had happened. She would have caught the next plane to America, but knowing I felt claustrophobic when Mum was around, Michelle convinced her to wait until I woke. When I did, and finally plucked up the nerve to return one of Mum's many messages, I told her I would be heading to Melbourne and she could pick me up when I was discharged.

I watched as Mum clasped the expensive handbag I'd bought for her and tapped her kitten heels against the carpet. She used to tap her toes when I handed her a bad school report, or when the smell of Jimmy's habit lingered in his room, or when Dad didn't come home at night.

'He's working late,' she'd say when she kissed my forehead and tucked me into bed. Then I would fall asleep to the sounds of the pitter-patter of Mum's feet on the kitchen floor.

I stopped at the end of the hall, about three feet behind her. 'Hi, you.'

She spun around with her hands in the air and a large open-mouthed smile stretched across her pale face. She wrapped her arms around me and kissed my cheek. 'Oh, Ruby honey.'

Our family had put her through a lot, and I was partially to blame for the stress lines that sank into her forehead, and the greys that peeked through her flawless, blow-waved, black hair.

'Dad and Jimmy wanted to come too, but I didn't want to overwhelm you.'

'Overwhelm me?'

'Well, should I say…?'

'It's okay,' I pulled her in for another hug, to ease the tension.

My mother and I were opposites. She was happy running errands for the family, scrubbing floors and baking scones between soap opera marathons and yoga moves. She had no career goals or pipedreams. She was an only child and had lived with her parents in a small Queensland town before meeting my dad in a Melbourne pub while celebrating her graduation with girlfriends – the same friends she continued to meet at an annual yoga retreat.

Dad was studying law at the time, and after he graduated, he got a job at his uncle's firm in Rockford – a small gold-mining town in central Victoria. About ten-thousand people lived in the town, which was formed on the back of the gold rush in the late 1800s. It had one of the only active underground goldmines left in Australia, operated by about five hundred employees, who were often seen drinking pints at the pubs, punting at the races, or cat-calling anything in heels from their car windows. Mum had said the town wouldn't have had two legs to stand on if it weren't for the miners, but she warned me to keep my distance. They were trouble, as were tradies and male nurses. 'Why would a man want to give sponge baths and wipe bottoms?'

'Why would a woman want to do it?' I'd asked in return. She never had an answer.

She wanted me to meet someone in my own industry, or else in the corporate sector. She wanted someone handsome, with brains and motivation. Like Dad, she used to say, until I got a little older and wiser.

My parents married when Mum was twenty-two and they moved into a small two-bedroom unit. They had me the next year, then Mum and Dad split up. Mum had told me later that it was because she was exhausted and lonely and took out her frustrations on Dad, eventually pushing him away. Dad moved in with his ageing uncle but returned to Mum six months later, and they had Jimmy shortly after.

Following their reunion, Mum tried her best to make our family seem picture perfect to outsiders. She relished my fame and flew overseas with her friends to see me in my first Broadway performance. When I gave up musicals for film roles, she organised parties at home or private viewings at cinemas in Melbourne – for the few movies that made it that far.

So the scandal would have torn her apart. The laughter and whispers, the pity-laced nods from strangers, the headlines, the pictures. She would have wept as she read about 'another out-of-control actress' suffering at her own hands, causing commotion on a movie set and being forced to get professional help. Hardly news in the entertainment world, but juicy enough to sell magazines. Funny enough, I never got a cut of the profits. It would have come in handy.

But whatever shame or embarrassment Mum had in the aftermath, she managed to push it aside to drive over two hundred kilometres from Rockford to pick me up from the hospital that I was admitted to once I landed in Melbourne. Mum kept her chin up high and smiled as she soaked up my cold embrace.

'It's been a wet summer so far,' she said as we walked out past the two stalky security guards.

I threw my jacket over my head but remembering it was genuine leather, shoved it back under my arm and let my hair get drenched as we dashed to the car.

The windshield wipers struggled to keep pace with the downpour. Our breathing, the potholes on the road, the tapping of Mum's fingers against the steering wheel – together they sounded like a steam train tearing through my aching head. I wanted a painkiller for the throbbing but resisted to avoid a lecture. I sensed the questions swirling behind Mum's worried eyes.

I turned the radio on and stared out the window, hoping the music would ease the pain. It all sounded muddled to me as I watched each white line that divided the highway pass us by. With a warm finger, I traced a raindrop from the top of the passenger window to the bottom where it spread out like a flowing river. At times I felt the tyres slide effortlessly above road puddles, like skates on ice.

Mum's voice was a steady distant murmur, louder than the hum of the radio but fading under the blow of the wind and the heavy rain.

For a while the rain eased and her voice projected. When I didn't shift my head or flinch my eyes, she reached over and turned the volume down. 'You know, it'll be just like old times. It'll be fun. You'll be back in your old room, too. I moved out all my yoga gear and DVD's. I can do that in the shed.'

'You could have left it, Mum. I'm only staying for three months.'

'Personally'—she raised her hand to her chest—'I don't think it's wise to go back to New York so soon. You need time for yourself, to reflect, to have a change of pace.'

'Regardless, you could have left your yoga stuff in the bedroom.'

'Well, it's just how you left it. Nothing has changed otherwise. Oh, except for a coat of paint. I painted it last year. The white walls were so boring. Yellow's more fun. Like sunshine.'

I didn't say much else for the rest of the drive. I wouldn't have gotten a word in if I'd tried. Mum rambled on about how much Rockford had changed and how she barely recognised anyone she passed on the streets. She told me that Jimmy had lost his job recently, but he hadn't broken the news to Dad. She said he spent a lot of time in his room with his guitar, playing along to rock music, or as she put it: 'a bunch of grown men who dress up, wear make-up and scream and cuss.' When she wasn't speaking about the grave concerns she held for Jimmy's future, she spoke about downward dogs, vanilla slices, petunias and rose bushes. Everything and anything but New York.

I'd forgotten about the vibrant golden fields lining the narrow road into Rockford. The town, on the other hand, was exactly as I remembered. After Mum's speech about the town's epic transformation, I had expected sky rails and hover cars, but gum trees still framed the main streets, though they had grown larger. Rockford remained the same, but I still felt like a foreigner passing through.

I stayed tight-lipped as I people watched. They walked from one side to another without having to dodge a single car. Women sat out front of the local café's, sipping flat whites, seemingly enjoying each other's company, their phones nowhere to be seen. Neighbours chatted over white picket fences, kids were on their bikes and miners stood in small groups, puffing on cigarettes outside the pub. No high-rise apartments, yellow taxis or street vendors. I wound the window down and took in a deep breath of fresh air.

'Sam said business is going really good.' Mum looked out her window. 'She gets all the miners there after the shifts during the week, then on Saturday's it's a mixed crowd. I've been there a time or two for a jive with the girls. Have you spoken to Sam lately?'

'A jive or two?' I raised an eyebrow but didn't turn my head. 'And no. Not for a while now.' I thought about it for a second, then let out a quiet laugh of disbelief.

'What's so funny?'

'Sam bought a pub,' I said. 'Talk about pouring petrol on a fire.'

'She's been on the straight and narrow for a while,' Mum said. 'Actually, it would do you good to catch up with her.'

THREE

We pulled up to the red brick house that lodged a wealth of my childhood memories. Black shutters still framed the windows and potted plants hung above the veranda.

When Dad's uncle died, we'd moved into his home and Dad took over the firm. The house was the only double storey on the quiet street, set amongst gum trees, and nature strips too narrow to park a car on. When we had visitors, they parked on the front lawn, much to Mum's dismay. In New York City, having a front lawn was unheard of, let alone parking on it.

Dad eventually saved enough money to grant my and Jimmy's wish of putting a pool in the backyard, leaving little room for a lush lawn or vegetable garden. Mum decided to keep a small area beside the house and the neighbour's picket fence for her rose bushes and fruit trees. She insisted, in fact. She wanted fresh flowers on her table and lemons in the fruit bowl. When her garden couldn't grant her wishes in the off season, she cheated by buying them at the Dixon Market.

The picket fence donned a fresh coat of white paint, bluestone pavers formed a path to the front door and the hedges along the neighbour's rendered facade were perfectly trimmed.

The property to the left of Mum and Dad's was a stark contrast. The red bricks looked more like a faded brown, a thick layer of dust coated the windows, weeds sprouted through the dead garden beds and, like a hunched woman struggling to carry a heavy basket, the branches of a large lemon tree hung in a losing battle to hold their fruit. The lemons that had broken free lay battered and half-eaten in the overgrown grass.

'Mrs Williams died a few years ago.' Mum looked to the unkempt yard. 'A young man moved in, a relative presumably.'

'I didn't know she had any family.'

Mrs Williams' husband had died when I was about six. The widow would only leave the house to fetch the mail or grab some groceries from the milk bar a couple streets away. I didn't recall seeing one visitor in all the years I lived next door.

'Apparently, she did. I don't see him much, though. A miner I'm assuming. I'm guessing he's just as much of a recluse as the old bat was.'

'Mum!'

'What? Strange woman she was. And look at how he's kept her yard. Atrocious. I've thought about complaining to the council.'

Her attention shifted to Dad, who stood in the open doorway, hands on hips and dressed in a three-piece grey suit. His thick eyebrows were groomed and his wide nose looked a little less prominent since he'd shaved his upper lip. Thankfully all I inherited from him was his olive complexion.

I got out of the car, expecting a swarm of cameras to flash from behind the bushes or for someone to call out 'Anna'. Instead I was greeted with silence, then an awkward hug and a pat on the back.

'Good to see you, kiddo.'

'Hey, Dad.'

I stood straight as he moved his hands to my shoulders, extended his arms and looked me up and down. 'Well, well.'

I assumed a lecture was coming, or some words of wisdom, but Mum cleared her throat, prompting Dad to move his hand to the small of my back and lead me inside. 'Welcome back. It's been too long.'

Mum followed us inside.

The overbearing scent of roast lamb mixed with the subtle aroma of a vanilla candle reminded me of every Sunday evening during my youth. Everything was in the same place: my white china dish under the candle; the brass clock on the wall; the expensive woven basket next to the entrance table that Mum forbid us to use for our shoes, scarves, or anything, really – it served no purpose but to look good and waste space.

'I see everything still has its place.'

'I've always said, there's comfort in the familiar,' Mum closed the door.

I walked past Dad, though the small entry and into the kitchen. It had a window overlooking the front yard, perfectly polished hardwood floors and dark oak cupboards. When I was younger, Mum would appear from over my shoulder whenever I pulled those cupboards open without using the handle. She'd wipe off any trace of fingerprints with a cloth, which I swore she stored in her bra in case the need arose. Any signs of life in our small house would be criminal.

I dragged my hand along the large family dining table and peered into the adjoining living room. The cushions had been fluffed, a knitted throw was folded over the armchair and the television remotes were stacked neatly on top of a collection of hardcover books on art. I doubt they had ever been opened.

An Australian soap opera was on the television, the sound muted.

'This show is still running?'

Dad huffed. 'Unfortunately, yes. Your mother has it set to come on every day at the same time. It's terrible. Same story lines all the time, new characters. It's a load of crap. Has a cult following of simple-minded people.'

'Oh, come on now,' Mum said. 'It's entertainment.'

'I rest my case,' Dad murmured.

I stretched my neck to see out the living room window into the backyard, hoping to catch a glimpse of Jimmy, but when I heard the creak of his door upstairs, I walked back to the entrance.

His skinny body swam in oversized jeans and a black t-shirt. His eyes looked like glossy, black shadows under his messy brown hair.

His stubble scratched my lips as I kissed him on the cheek. 'Jimmy! What's this shit on your face?'

He laughed, squinted and rubbed his thumb and index finger over his chin. 'This? Chicks love this.'

'Oh yeah, they're just lining up,' Dad said.

'I bet they do.' I gently punched Jimmy on the shoulder.

'How was—'

'Rehab? Great. I really got to know my true self and face my inner demons. It was riveting. A true spiritual journey.' I rolled my eyes and Jimmy smirked.

'I was going to ask how the trip back was, but whatever.'

'She had to sit in economy for the first time in her life,' Dad said. 'I'm sure it was an eye-opener.'

'Now, that's enough, please,' Mum shot.

'Welcome back,' I grumbled as we walked up the steps, leaving Mum and Dad to collect my bags from the car. I stopped at the landing. 'There was no turbulence, no paparazzi, and no delays, so the flight was fine. Driving from Melbourne to Rockford with Mum is another story. You can only imagine.'

'No, I can't. And I won't. The past week she kept saying she didn't want to say anything about the situation.'

'The situation, hey?' I shook my head. 'She can't even bring herself to say it.'

I pushed open the door to my bedroom to see everything was as I'd left it, except, as Mum mentioned, the paint colour.

'It's like you're stepping back in time.'

'Thanks for the commentary, you bogan.'

'Ah, so you aren't all Americano, after all,' Jimmy mimicked me in a terrible American accent. 'There's still a bit of Aussie left in you.'

I laughed, though I had picked up a slight American twang over the years. 'Piss off. I don't speak like that.'

'There it is,' he shouted as he walked to his bedroom. 'You bloody rippa.'

I closed the door and set my handbag on the single bed, which was draped with a pink quilt and piled with white pillows. There was little space for many more furnishings in the room – only a tallboy and a mirror next to a little wooden desk – the one I sat at when I was eight and etched out my plan. Old photos in painted frames hung on the wall – a couple of professional shots of Jimmy and me, some pictures of Sam and me posing in our netball outfits, and polaroids of old friends I'd lost contact with over the years.

The Polaroid camera I'd got as a present in my teenage years was on the desk. I sat near my pillow, pointed the camera at myself and snapped. I was surprised when it spat out a photo. It still worked after all these years. I stared at the image. My brown curls hung on my shoulders, the few freckles exposed on my straight nose, my lips dry and dark circles jumped on my dull skin.

I pinned the photo next to the ones of Sam and me then walked to the window, pulled back one side of the sheer curtains and looked over to Mrs Williams' house, as I had often done growing up. I'd watch through one of her window's as she'd brew a cup of tea in her kitchen or I'd see her rock in her chair through a window at the rear of the house. With curlers in her hair and glasses resting on the end of her nose, she would sit in that chair and knit every night. I used to think she was so lonely, that she had no idea what she was missing by shutting everyone out. But I understood it now. How serene it must have been.

I looked from the kitchen- decked with wooden cabinetry and yellow walls- to the back room to see a home gym had replaced the rocking chair. A man walked by the window. I flinched and shuffled back to hide behind the wall. Curious, I inched my head forward until I could see him again. He was lying on the bench seat, pulling the lat bar down to his broad, bare chest. He did this several times, slowing between each rep until his tattooed arms shook. He sat up, grabbed a towel from near his feet, and wiped his jaw and shaven head.

I held the curtain by my face, but he looked up to my window. Caught! I thrust the curtain closed and threw my back against the wall again.

I spent the next few days in my room, on the couch or sitting near the pool, looking through magazine clippings of myself that Mum had carefully cut out, laminated and tucked into a folder.

I sat on Jimmy's bedroom floor while he smoked his joints and strummed his guitar. I laughed when, in an attempt to conceal the bitter scent, he sprayed his room with an air freshener that smelled like musk and mothballs and did more damage to the nostril than good.

Almost a week into my stay, after my skin darkened from the scorching sun and I grew weary with boredom, I plucked up the courage to leave the house and brave the townsfolk. I wore my hair up and hid my bare face under a silk scarf to mask me from paparazzi who might be lurking, waiting to pounce on the short walk to The Night Owl. There were none.

Despite it being mid-afternoon on a Wednesday, heavy bass from classic rock sounded through the dark wooden entry of the pub. No-one lifted their head at the door chimes as I slipped inside. The carpets were sticky and had a strong stench of stale beer.

Men, I assumed to be miners, gathered around the pool tables, a group of five sat at a table with pints in their hands, watching the American hockey on an overhead screen. Two women stood nearby sharing a laugh.

Then there was the guy sitting at the bar. I recognised him. The shaven head and tattooed arms. He wore a white t-shirt, and like most Aussies in the midst of summer, had glowing tanned skin. Two of his fingers wrapped loosely around a glass of dark liquor and he stared ahead. He looked at his glass, bit his lip, took a drink, then continued staring.

'Ruby!'

I startled at the boisterous voice, turning away from the guy at the bar and towards the voluptuous woman beside me. Sam was a healthier version of the last time I'd seen her. She'd covered her cheeks with a bronzer, hiding the small scars she had from neglecting to look after her skin during her tumultuous teenage years. Any doubts I'd had about Sam wanting to see me were crushed when she wrapped her arms around me.

She pulled back and placed her hands on my bony shoulders. 'I should have come to see you. I just couldn't see you in… there. I didn't know if you wanted visitors or anything. I don't—'

'It's alright,' I whispered. 'I'm alright. I didn't belong in there anyway.'

I didn't. But Michelle had said it would be good for my image. 'How can we get anyone to cast you after that?' she said at my hospital bed. 'You need to do this. No ifs, ands or buts. Just show up, do the time, and get over it. Think of it as a luxury getaway.'

'Except it's not a luxury.'

'That's right. Because you can't afford it.'

'Right.'

'Time to yourself is always a luxury. Perhaps I'll check myself in too.' Michelle's thumbs were hastily pressing buttons on her mobile. 'Melbourne has a few options, surely one will suit.'

'Melbourne?'

'Melbourne,' she looked to me for a moment, studied my face, then went back to texting. 'We just spoke about this yesterday.'

'Yeah, but I didn't think you meant immediately.'

'What did you think I meant? You sure as hell can't spend another week here. The paps will go nuts. I'll arrange for your bags to be packed and sent to Rockford.'

I rested my face in my hands. 'This seems heavy-handed.'

'You trust me?' Michelle put her phone in her handbag and stood, her posture perfect in three-inch stilettos.

'I always do.'

'Then stop questioning me.'

Sam's voice broke through my memory. 'So?' Her eyebrows were raised, waiting for a response. 'You okay?'

'Sorry, what?'

'I asked if you can have a cider. Are you allowed to drink?'

I was surprised she still remembered my drink of choice. 'I better not. Not yet. Maybe a lemon lime and bitters? It's been a while since I had one of those.'

'Damn, girl. You had me so worried.' She walked behind the bar, still several feet away from the tattooed man, and poured a drink. 'What did New York do to you?'

I shrugged.

'Oh, well. Been there, done that. Not to New York, obviously. You know what I'm saying. And look at me now.' She slid the drink to me, raised her hands in the air and winked. 'Owner of the most popular pub in Rockford, baby!'

If Sam had told me years ago she wanted to buy a bar, I would have punched her on the shoulder and told her to wake up to herself. We had that sort of bond. One we didn't think could ever be broken.

We grew up together. Sam had asked me if I wanted to jump rope with her in the playground, on our first day of school. She was the first person I'd ever had over to my house for a sleepover, where we ate until we felt sick and laughed until our bellies ached. She was the person who helped me get ready for my first date with my first crush, and she was the person who patted me on the back and wiped away my tears, when he broke my heart. She was also the person who taught me how to sneak out of the house when I was thirteen and the first person I shared a beer with. Many years later, when we would break curfew together at parties, she was the one who would walk me home and then hold my hair back when I vomited into Mum's potted plants. We shared a love of netball, boys and parties. We did everything together.

Then our lives took different turns: while I spent most of my time after school in acting classes or at the gym, she hung out with people she met through her shady older cousin who had a 'bad boy' reputation. I would be studying scripts and she would be smoking cigarettes and listening to grunge music in a stranger's basement. She went from cigarettes to weed to cocaine and almost anything else on offer.

I had the odd joint but each puff burned and made me feel sick, so when she offered me blow, I refused.

In a matter of months, I watched Sam's beautiful complexion become aged with spots, scabs and dark circles under her eyes. Her long glossy hair hung limp, dry and knotted down to the small of her back.

She left me at parties to get high in a room of people she had just met. She stopped going to school and started working at a petrol station to make money to feed her habit. She racked up a slow and steady debt she couldn't repay. I watched her cry from fear. I watched her beg for hits from people we didn't know well. I watched her dignity crumble.

Her parents knew they had lost control. They threatened to kick her out, but they never did. Instead they waited up for her at night, cooked her breakfast in the morning and drove her to work when she chose to show up.

Her problem continued to get worse. One evening, Sam gave me directions and told me to meet her at the house. When I arrived, she was standing behind the hedges near the side of the house with a group of guys.

Sam waved and called to me, then grabbed my hand and pulled me inside. Within the hour, she was moaning about how she needed to get high but didn't know anyone at the house who could deliver the goods.

I convinced her to do a couple shots of tequila with me instead, but after the burn subsided and the buzz wore off, she was back looking to score.

When I was ready to go home, I tried to find Sam to say goodbye and spotted her in the kitchen, talking to a bulky, bearded guy. She whispered in his ear and he smiled a toothless, preying grin. He held a beer in one hand and grabbed her ass with the other before the two of them ducked into the bathroom.

I was used to seeing her sneak off with older, unfamiliar men to snort a line before returning to the party with remnants of powder on her nostrils and a bounce in her step. But that evening was different. She emerged from the bathroom sniffling and rubbing her nose, and the man followed behind her, zipping up his pants. They walked separate ways into different rooms and continued to drink and laugh like nothing had happened. My heart sank. Not just because, at that moment, I learned how bad her problem was, but because I knew I had lost my best friend. The Sam I knew was long gone.

I told her I thought she had a problem, but she didn't listen, so I stopped making plans with her. Instead, we would call each other on weekends to discuss where we had been or what we had seen. Most of her stories began with, 'I was so high last night,' or 'I can't remember a thing,' or 'I just got home, I am so bloody tired.'

A few months after I went to New York, Sam told me she stopped getting high. I kept in touch with her through emails and texts. She went back to school while I started making a mark on Broadway.

About a week after Sam graduated, she got drunk and sent a message telling me how proud she was for being able to get wasted without getting high. I told her I was proud of myself for landing a lead role in a movie. It was in that conversation that we realised a twenty-hour flight wasn't the only thing that distanced us.

We remained connected though social media. I liked her pictures. She liked mine. I posted videos of red carpet events and premiers; she posted ones of her doing keg stands.

Eventually, sometime in those years that divided us, Sam got a serious boyfriend, cut back her partying ways and, as a casual drinker trying to prove a point, bought a bar. And I, in trying to catch my breath in a suffocating industry, had an accidental overdose, got fired and moved back to Australia to live with my parents.

'You look happy, Sam.'

She poured herself a water, walked around the bar and took a seat next to me.

'I am. Got a roof over my head, money in my pocket, oh, and a pretty cool boyfriend. You'll have to meet him while you're here. How long are you here?'

'A few months.'

'Think you can last that long away from the bright lights of NYC?'

'I'll find out, I guess. I'm sure it won't be long until the paparazzi track me down here.'

She drank her water, sat the glass on the bar, then rested her hands on her spread knees and pursed her lips. 'You're not in New York anymore, Dorothy. You're in Rockford now, girl. Don't worry about tabloids because no-one here cares. They don't care about your money, your headlines, your... you know'—she circled her finger in the air, then dropped it back in her lap—'your episode. No. Body. Cares.'

The door chimes rang, and I turned to see the tattooed neighbour had gone. He'd left a twenty-dollar bill underneath his empty glass. Sam grabbed the money and a cloth from behind the bar, wiped under the glass and placed the money in the till. 'Nobody cares about all that celebrity bullshit in Rockford. You can do whatever you want here.'

I stared at the door for a moment, then turned back to Sam.

'You can do anything,' she said, 'anything but him.'

'What?' I laughed, embarrassed.

'Busted.' She smiled. 'Checking out the prey already? Rockford won't have anything on the men you've pounced on in the concrete jungle, you minx, you.' She curled her hand up by her face and swiped it, like a cat.

I shook my head. 'For one, I think you would be highly disappointed if I revealed my list to you.'

She leaned in, resting her chin on her hand and raised her eyebrows. 'Oh, do tell.'

'That's confidential.'

Sam huffed.

'And two, I wasn't checking him out. I think he's my parents neighbour. I was just wondering what a guy is doing in here alone, this time of day, drinking rum. Seems sad.'

'And we should judge?' Sam straightened her back and tossed the cloth over her shoulder. 'And it's Scotch. He comes in often, has a couple scotches on the rocks and then leaves. He doesn't say much. He's a bit of a loner. He works at the mine and, by all accounts, he's shady. Hot, but shady.'

I'd never been good at picking out the good men from the bad, and I'd never had a relationship in New York that lasted more than six months. I dated them all – the arrogant actor who cheated on me several times, the director who promised he could further my career but cut me after he had enough of sleeping with me, the model who spent more time at the hair salon than I did, the loud-mouth, the loner, the over-achiever, the under-achiever, the secretly-gay, the womaniser. No-one came close to my first, and only love. Lucas had sent the benchmark, and no-one else compared.

'I'm not looking,' I insisted. 'I've only been here a week. I'm leaving in eleven.'

♥

FOUR

I struggled to fall asleep in the silence that night, and as soon as I did, I woke to chirping birds. I felt lost without appointments or meetings. I had no direction. No-one to tell me what to wear or eat, where to go, what time to be there. I hadn't talked to Michelle all week.

I missed the cameras and the fanfare. In New York, there were mornings when I would peek through my apartment blinds, before leaving for gym sessions or production meetings, and scan the narrow streets below to pick out who was waiting for me.

I had come to recognise many of the usuals who knew my favourite café and shops. They sat on park benches, stoops or leaned against the brownstone buildings, a camera dangling in one hand, usually a cigarette or mobile in the other, until I emerged. Some days I hated it. I wanted to leave the house with a bare face and messy hair or to be able to buy tampons in private. But sometimes, when I questioned my performances, or wondered if anyone even cared about who I was or what I did, I relished any attention thrown my way

To the Rockford locals, I just used to be 'one of them'. I grew up riding my bike on back roads and playing netball in my spare time. I had posters of footy players on my walls and idolised Olivia Newton John and Kylie Minogue. I was a small-town girl who'd moved away, prepared to jump through hoops while chasing dreams, only to end up falling flat and returning to nurse my wounds.

I missed New York, hungered for all its busyness – the sea of yellow cabs, the rush of people, the eclectic culture. I missed people-watching in Central Park. On the odd day I had nothing on, I would hide behind some silk scarf and sunnies, buy a sugar-free soy latte at my usual spot and then take a seat next to a stranger and watch couples walk by hand in hand, or families ride past on bikes. Some would set up their chessboards and challenge others to games in competitions, which I never had time to see through. Others would put up a sign by a basket and dance, sing or show off their quirky skills in a shameless effort to entertain while making a quick buck.

Funny enough, since returning to Rockford, I missed the very thing I tried to escape while in that popular park. I missed feeling important – whether it was at casting calls, or on set, or even at the gym. Yoga with my mother did little to curb my Big Apple craving. But in the last few days, I had developed somewhat of a loose routine. After waking at whatever hour the birds chirped, I did some exercise in the backyard, ate some breakfast, had a shower, then wandered around aimlessly for the remainder of the day.

Mum felt the need to give a running commentary of whatever she had done, was doing or planned to do for the day. Yoga was the only time Mum welcomed silence between us. She insisted we stay focused and relaxed. I had trouble turning my brain off, but she closed her eyes and was so easily taken somewhere else. I watched as the intensity disappeared from her face and her shoulders dropped, like she had been relieved of the weight of the world. I wondered what or who she thought of.

'Ruby, I think you would love the retreat we go on,' she said to me after one backyard session.

'Yeah?' I wiped my face with my towel.

'I would really like for you to join us.'

I raised an eyebrow, desperately trying to think of an excuse not to go. 'I dunno, mum. I...'

'We are going in two months, while you are still in Australia. It's worked out perfectly.'

'What a coincidence,' I smiled, trying not to offend. 'But I don't know if a yoga retreat is...'

'It will be a great opportunity to have some mother-daughter time. You know, without the men around.'

I raised my shoulders, shook my head slowly, then nodded. 'Well, okay then.'

'Really?' Mum sounded surprised.

I took a deep breath. 'Really.'

'Oh wonderful!' She clapped her hands together then gave me a hug. 'I can't wait.'

After we changed, mum continued her desperate attempt to bond and asked me to go with her to the Dixon Farmers' Market, which I used to tag along to and enjoy when I was a little girl. Dixon was only about five minutes' drive down a narrow dirt track. There wasn't much there except for a bakery, a fish and chip shop and a racetrack – where the market was held when the races weren't on. Mum would hand me a five-dollar note and I'd wait in line for fresh hot jam donuts and a freshly squeezed lemonade, then find a spot on the grass and inhale both while she picked a bouquet of flowers for the week and bought fresh bread and fruit.

The market's diversity hadn't changed much since I had last been. I recognised the woman behind the daisies and tulips stall and wondered if she remembered me. She looked older, was hunched over, but her eyes and smile remained the same.

'Those flowers are lovely, dear. Aren't they?'

'They are,' I said. 'I'll take this bunch, please.' The selection at the market was like David to the Goliath of Manhattan's markets, but they would do.

Mum stood nearby, holding her bag to her chest and sniffing the roses.

'Don't get any, Mum. These are for you.' I raised the bouquet towards her and she tilted her head.

'Oh, Ruby, that's very sweet of you.' She smiled. 'Thank you, Mrs Lopes. See you next week.'

Mum joined me and waved at the old lady who was looking me over as though she was trying to recall who I was. We navigated our way through the large crowd of locals who swung their shopping bags from their arms and jerked on the chains of their curious dogs.

Mum waved or nodded at the occasional acquaintance. I felt the stares and heard the whispers of a few strangers as we rubbed against their shoulders in the narrow paths. While I missed the attention I had gotten in America, the mutters and eye rolls were a blunt reminder of why I had left. I grabbed the large sunnies off the top of my head and lowered them over my eyes.

It was then, through the dark tint of my lenses that the man from the bar stood out in the crowd. A baseball cap cast a shadow over his face as he sunk his teeth into the skin of a yellow pear. He walked quickly, so I kept my head down and hurried after him with Mum trying to keep pace beside me.

We both spun around at the sound of a young voice. 'Anna! Are you Anna Johns?'

A girl, aged about thirteen, stood wide-eyed as though she had just stumbled upon a hidden gem. Braces clad her crooked teeth and a pink headband wrapped around her curly hair. Her mother hung back a few feet back, arms crossed and lips pursed.

'Yes, I am.' I looked down at her and smiled

'Can I get a photo with you?'

'You don't want to bother her, darling. We really should get going,' her mother said.

Michelle had warned me about getting photos, but looking at this young girl was like looking at my eight-year-old self, eagerly waiting by the backstage door.

'Would you settle for an autograph?'

The mother's lips curled slightly. 'Yes, I don't think we need a picture.'

I grabbed a serviette from the donut van behind me, bent down so our heads were level, grabbed a pen from my bag and signed the name Anna.

The girl smiled and thanked me, then ran to her unamused mother.

Mum wrapped her arm around me. 'Her mother seemed rapt.'

'Oh, I could have slapped the horrid look off her smug face.'

She rubbed my arm.

'How quickly you can go from a role model to an international disgrace,' I muttered.

'Oh, Ruby. Give it time. It's still fresh in everyone's mind. Things will change.'

As I peered through the crowd, wondering how many other parents were trying to hide their daughters from me, I spotted the neighbour walk out the gates.

I barely recognised my reflection and hoped others wouldn't either. Scattered chunks of my brown hair were stuck to the sides of the basin, and a box of bleach sat amongst the rubbish in the bin. Scissors rested near the taps, with frays of hair dangling from their blades.

I ran my fingers through my short hair. It was a big change. Michelle would have a fit. But strangely, I felt reinvigorated.

Back in my room, I flicked on the light and went to shut the blinds. The neighbour was on the gym bench again, repeating the same move as last time, his arms visibly shaking with each rep. Once he finished, he sat up, wiped his forehead and looked up to me. Does he know I'm watching?

His stare was intense and firm, without shame or pity. His knees were bent, slightly apart, and he rested his elbows on them and folded his hands together. His face didn't move.

I reached to pull my hair over my shoulder, but was quickly reminded that inches of my identity were now making their way through sewage pipes under Rockford. I dropped my hand back to my hip and looked back at the neighbour. I hadn't been watched like that before, not without agenda. Not without casting hopes or tabloid deals.

He stood and looked to the floor as he walked to the window, then lifted his eyes to mine again and held my gaze.

For a moment, I stopped breathing. I was onstage, and he was my audience. I had his undivided attention and I froze, only exhaling after he dropped the blinds.

FIVE

'I like it. You look good as a blonde. Maybe even a few years younger. Like some sort of pop star.'
'A pop star?'
'Or an actress.'
'I am an actress'
'Right. Well, my point exactly. It suits you'

I scrunched my face and pulled at my hair. 'This was a stupid move, wasn't it?'

'No, definitely not. You look hot.' Sam thrust up her finger like she used to do in school every time she knew the answer to a question. 'You look heaps younger.'

'So a younger, hotter version of my former self. Could I be mistaken for a woman in my twenties?' I sipped my latte and peered at Sam as she loudly slurped her milkshake through a red-striped straw. I had spent most of my life seeking approval for my looks, and I rarely got it. I was either too thin, too fat, too old, too young. I was never good enough.

Sam sat across from me on the deck of a quaint cafe. It was small by Rockford terms yet huge by New

York's. The sun hit her back, blocking me from the heat, but casting a warm light around us.

'Definitely. You look hot.'

I smiled. 'Are you working tonight?'

'Yup. Tonight, tomorrow night, the night after.' She brushed her hands together and the croissant crumbs fell from her palms and spread across her lap. 'You want a part-time gig?'

'I don't think I'm cut out for it, Sam.'

'Well, if you want to do something with yourself during your little staycation, you can pick up a few shifts. We need some spare hands.' She dusted the crumbs off her skirt.

'I'll keep it in mind.'

'God, I'm a mess.'

'Me and you both,' I laughed.

After I paid for her drink, I offered to give her a lift home. I had borrowed Dad's car while he was interstate on business. In a town where most people opted for utes and four-wheel drives, the decision to take Dad's Porsche wasn't the smartest in my new plan to stay incognito.

Sam ran her hands over the luxury leather interior as she sang along to a song I didn't know – a new Aussie band, perhaps. She rolled her window down and shook her head, long locks flying across her face. She didn't miss a word as she pulled strands from her mouth.

She reminded me of the girl I had grown up with, not the one I left behind. Sam didn't ask about my time away – the highs and the lows – and I didn't ask about hers. She didn't ask me about my hospital stay, how I felt about the headlines or why I changed my hair. I didn't owe her an explanation, and maybe that's why I felt comfortable around her. Maybe it was just nostalgia.

I stopped the car and watched as Sam flicked the door closed with her hip and bounce down the footpath and into her one-bedroom brick house. I looked at the blonde version of myself through the rear-view mirror, winked, changed the radio station, and drove away.

I was mid-lyric when I spotted a familiar woman in black heels and a matching dress, cradling a handbag. She was laughing with an older man outside a clothing shop.

A knot formed in my stomach as my mind raced back. High school. I was at my desk working out a maths problem when I heard my dad's name. I put my pencil down and leaned back to eavesdrop on the two girls behind me. They giggled as they spoke of Dad and another student's mother.

The same mother who I would see at after-school pickup. She wore expensive pearls, tight-fitting dresses and her lips were always painted in red. She'd congregate with a group of her friends outside their cars in the pick-up zone. When they weren't whispering stories to each other, they were laughing obnoxiously. She'd wave at all the passing parents. But she never waved at my mum. She didn't even give her a sideways glance.

I never asked Mum about it. I didn't have to. Her fingernails got shorter, her wrinkles got deeper and the toe tapping habit began.

This other woman was the initial cut in my slate of innocence. She was the realisation that the first man I ever loved wasn't the man I loved at all. He had gone from being my hero to a stranger. She was the reason my mother was so protective of me. Mum tried too hard to keep me busy, to keep me from being angry or jaded. She thought all her efforts had failed when Michelle broke the news.

The woman's face had been etched in the back of my mind for two decades, only finding her way to the forefront when she could be of use for a boxing session or a hate scene.

But seeing her in the flesh caught me off-guard – a quick jolt of my neck, a locked seatbelt tightening its grip, and I was slammed against the leather seat. In my rear-view mirror was a Ford Ranger, which had run up the back of Dad's car.

'Damn it!' I pulled the car to the side of the road and the large black ute followed. I rested my head in my hands, took a deep breath and opened the door.

The familiar neighbour stepped out. His piercing eyes fixated on mine as he walked over in his florescent jumper and heavy work boots, quietly inspected the few marks on the front of his ute, then scrunched his nose at the bent bumper and hanging headlight of Dad's Porsche.

'I'm so sorry,' I cringed.

'Who stops in the middle of the road?' His voice was deep and stern.

'I got distracted, I guess.' I held my hand over my eyebrow and tucked my head down, hoping none of the lurking nosy locals would take photos.

'Just distracted? So, you stopped in the middle of the road?' He scratched the top of his head. 'And I'm going to get done because I ran up your ass. And you're driving a Porsche. In Rockford?'

I ran my hand over the back of my neck, slightly annoyed he didn't ask if I was alright, slightly curious if he recognised me.

'It's my dad's, and I'll pay.'

'That explains it.'

'Explains what?'

He looked at me, smirked, shook his head and then grabbed his wallet. 'Let's just exchange details and get this over with. I'll cover it.'

'Well, you know where I live,' I laughed, hoping he would find some humour in the situation, but closed my eyes in embarrassment when he didn't reciprocate. I tucked my hands into my pockets. 'Ruby Jones.'

He didn't flinch as he tapped my name into his phone.

'Some know me as Anna. But my real name is Ruby.'

Again, he seemed unfazed.

'You don't know who I am?' I asked again.

'Yup. You're my neighbour. A rich little daddy's girl who goes by two names, likes to stare into windows, and can't drive, apparently.' He stared into his phone and I wondered if he was being sarcastically playful or brutally blunt.

'Well, you seem like a nice guy.'

He finally looked up.

'You know,' I said, 'I'd been stopped for a while. You had plenty of time to stop too.' I grabbed my phone. 'What's your details?'

He raised his eyebrow, paused, then tucked his phone back in his pocket.

'Jack McKercher.'

I put his number in my phone, and while he sat on the curb, I called a tow-truck. When I hung up, I sat next to him and crossed my arms on my knees and tapped my toes against the pavement. A fly circled around my head then landed on my cheek. I swatted at it and it moved on to one of the dandelions which were sprung up between the cracks on the footpath behind us. 'A tow-truck's on its way,' I said. 'I don't think I should be driving it to the panel beaters.'

'Probably right.'

'It shouldn't be long and you don't have to stay. You're obviously on your way to work.'

'I just left work and I have nowhere else to be. I'll wait.'

I felt this was his way of apologising for being such an arse minutes earlier. I steadied my tapping foot and shaky hands. The silence raised the tension and I couldn't hack it much longer. 'You know, you got me all wrong.'

'Yeah?'

'Yeah. I wasn't staring into your window. I was looking out mine and you just happened to be parading yourself in front of yours.'

He let out a laugh. 'Parading?'

'What do you call walking around shirtless and puffing out your chest?'

'Working out?'

'Anyway, I'm actually not a bad driver, and I'm not just some rich man's daughter.'

'You're a bit sensitive, too.'

I still couldn't read him. We sat in silence for another minute until the silence got to me again. 'You were at The Night Owl the other evening?'

'Yeah.'

'Do you go there often?'

He raised his chin slightly, then looked away. 'Sometimes.'

'Do you work around here?' I already knew the answer.

'At the mines.'

'Have you lived here long?'

'For a bit.' Jack stared ahead as he told me how he'd moved from Queensland to Rockford three years ago. He didn't tell me why, or who with, or much of anything else. He didn't seem to know who I was, what I had done, or care to find out.

The tow-truck appeared before I could dig deep and learn more about Jack.

'How are you going to get home?'

I looked at the Porsche connected to the back of the tow-truck. 'I'll walk. I like the exercise.'

'I'll drive you.' Jack didn't wait for me to reply before he opened his passenger door.

After a short drive in silence, he pulled past the white picket fence and stopped out front of my parent's driveway. 'Good luck with the car.'

'So, looks like I'll be car shopping soon.' Dad spun the spaghetti around his fork, a glass of red wine within arm's reach. Jimmy held a mobile in his left hand, trying to wrap his lips around a heaping mound of pasta too large for his small mouth. After a few failed attempts, he shook some strands loose and sucked in the rest, leaving a trail of dripping red sauce on his chin.

'That bad?' I asked Dad.

'That bad.'

'The main thing is that everyone is okay.' Mum bent over Dad's shoulder, shaking the parmesan jar onto his half-eaten dish.

'I know that. I'm only saying—'

'Well, don't.' Mum slammed the jar onto the table with such force that specks of cheese flew from the lid and landed on Dad's lap. 'That's what's important. That everyone is okay. Don't make a big fuss.'

Dad rolled his eyes and took a sip of red wine. I wanted to tell him that I'd been distracted by his old mistress. That the accident was an act of karma. Instead my unwavering eyes burned a hole in his olive skin until he sat his glass down and raised his eyes to mine.

'I'll buy you a new car, Dad.'

'It's fine, Ruby. I have enough money to buy myself a new car.' He threw a sideways glance at Mum, who firmly stared at her glass of water, a pitter-patter echoing on the floor beneath her. 'Maybe look after yourself, Ruby, before you start offering to look after me.'

I clenched my teeth and sunk my fingers into my thighs. Dad reached across the table, snatched Jimmy's phone from him and flung it to the ground. 'Get off your damn phone, Jimmy.' He readjusted the serviette on his lap and straightened his back. 'We're eating. As a family.'

Jimmy picked up his phone and shifted his hips as he tucked it in his pocket. He shuffled uncomfortably in his seat. His arms were thin and his skin pale. Small drips of spaghetti sauce stained his white, oversized t-shirt.

Dad cleared his throat. 'How's work, Jimmy?'

I bit my bottom lip and looked towards Mum. Her eyes widened when Jimmy didn't respond.

'I asked you a question, son,' Dad said.

'Dunno Dad... I haven't been there for a month.'

Mum jerked her chin forward. 'It wasn't his fault, Mark.'

Jimmy dropped into his seat and I looked across the table.

Dad set down his cutlery and took a deep breath. 'What do you mean, Jimmy?'

'He had the wrong roster,' Mum said. 'His manager was so disorganised.'

'I, uh, missed my shift, so they fired me.'

Dad pushed his chair back, screeching the legs against the floorboards and rattling his empty plate. God dammit, Jimmy. You are twenty-eight. Get a bloody job in the next week or else you can find somewhere else to stay. Stop getting high and maybe you can make something of yourself one day.' Dad turned to Mum. 'And you need to stop defending him. It's your fault he's the way he is. How long did you know about this?'

'Don't take it out on her.'

'Don't start with me, Jimmy.' Dad shook his finger and stormed off to the living room. 'How come the entire community respects me, but my own family doesn't? You have one week, Jimmy. One week.' He slinked into the sofa and turned the volume up on the television.

Jimmy shovelled more pasta.

I wondered how he was content to float along, living under Mum and Dad's roof, off their dollar, without any short-term goals or agenda? He hated work, he loved weed, movies and music. Just days before I'd left Rockford to pursue my dreams, he'd told me he wanted to buy a van, pack only a suitcase and a guitar and road trip across the country, busking when he needed money. We were sitting outside on the front steps of the veranda.

'Why don't you?'

A car drove by, and a small Jack Russell chased behind, barking madly.

'Have you ever seen a dog actually catch the car it's chasing?' he asked.

'I don't think so.'

'What do you supposed would happen if it did?'

'I don't know, Jimmy. It would be one happy pup.'

'I don't think so,' he said.

I gave him a look. 'Why?'

'The way I see it, there are two outcomes: it keeps running and running until it loses steam and returns home with its tail between its legs, feeling like it's failed miserably...'

I laughed. 'And the second one?'

'If it reaches it, it most likely will come unstuck. You know, get caught up under the tyre and break its leg, if it's lucky. Or if it's not, get crushed under the weight.'

I didn't say anything.

Looking at Jimmy now, in front of his empty bowl of pasta, I knew which of us had chased the car, and which of us was too afraid to.

'Jimmy,' – I asked – 'would you consider working at The Night Owl?'

He raised his eyes and mumbled. 'Maybe.'

'Yeah, you're interested? I met with Sam and she said they need people. Maybe you can come with me to ask what you can do?'

'Yeah, alright.' He rubbed his forearm across his lips.

'Okay, let's go tomorrow.'

SIX

Several miners filled the bar seats in The Night Owl. They were straight from work and not yet showered, dirt staining their faces and burying into the dark or silver hair of whoever was young enough to still have some. Young girls, barely eighteen, sipped cocktails nearby. A few people stood around the two pool tables. Their laughter rumbled above the music blaring from the 1950s-style jukebox behind them. The televisions were off and the lights dimmed.

Jimmy and I bumped elbows with a group of beer-drinking middle-aged men who, unlike the miners, looked a little cleaner but a tad more drunk. One man turned to watch me walk past, and I thought he may have known who I was, despite me wearing no make-up and having bleached hair. He whistled, they laughed, then I thought I heard, above all the clamour, the words 'Anna Johns.'

Jimmy grabbed my hand and pulled me towards Sam, who stood behind the busy bar staff juggling pints and cash. Jimmy looked handsome. Despite the layer of gel on his combed-back hair, his freshly shaven face highlighted his narrow nose and sharp chin. He wore a black, buttoned-up shirt and dark jeans, and his cologne was strong and musky.

'Well, look at you, pussycat. What did you drag in?'

'Hey, friend.' I took a seat in front of her and quickly scanned the room for Jack, but couldn't see him at the end of the bar.

'Little Jimmy boy. Not so little anymore. Haven't seen you in a while.'

'He's after a job.' I leaned in. The smell of beer quickly overpowered Jimmy's cologne. There was another man behind the bar, clad in black with a towel draped over his shoulder, serving half-drunk patrons. Another bartender stood next to him. She was a short woman with long blonde hair tucked neatly in a high ponytail. She had fake eyelashes, bright lips and wore a tight t-shirt which showed off her ample chest. I caught Jimmy staring and slyly moved my elbow into his ribcage. He stood straight and averted his stare to Sam.

'Yeah, anything.'

'Don't sound too eager.' Sam rolled her eyes and glanced at the two bartenders, then back at Jimmy. 'We do need someone to collect glasses, wipe tables – that sort of thing. And to do dishes.'

'Dishes?'

'Yeah. We don't lick them clean though, dish licker. We wash them. With real soap. And water. And a big machine called a dishwasher.'

'Yup.'

'Can you handle it?'

'Yup.'

She threw him a towel. 'The blonde bartender is Kate. She's taken so stop eyeballing her.'

Jimmy looked to Kate, who was oblivious to Sam's lecture.

'We wear black, we show up on time, we don't drink on the job, and you get two fifteen-minute breaks per shift. Half hour for meals,' Sam continued. 'If you shit in the toilets, clean up your skids. You can start in the kitchen'—she paused— 'cleaning in it, not shitting in it.'

'Tonight?'

'You got other plans? We have a pile of glasses in the back and they aren't going to wash themselves.'

'Alright.' Jimmy scratched his hair. Sam jerked her head towards the kitchen, and Jimmy slumped his shoulders, dragging his feet to the door. 'Thanks, Sam. I think.'

'No worries.'

'Thanks... for that.' I pointed to the kitchen door behind her.

'Anything for a friend.' She opened a coke, poured it into a glass, slid it across the bar, then motioned for me to follow her to an empty booth. As we sat, I spotted Jack entering. He slid into a stool at the end of the bar, and without saying a word, Kate took him a scotch on the rocks.

'You're checking out that loner again,' Sam said.

'We had a bit of a run-in.'

'Whaaaat? Define "run-in".'

I took a sip and forcefully swallowed the ice-cold drink then ran my tongue across the roof of my mouth until it felt warm again. Sam patiently waited. 'I got distracted in Dad's car, stopped in the middle of the road. He crashed into it.'

'Oh, damn. A run-in. Literally.' She covered her mouth as she laughed and snorted. 'Did he go off on you? Of all people in Rockford…'

'No, he was fine. Slightly annoyed, understandably, but he waited until the tow-truck came.'

I could tell by Sam's dubious stare that I hadn't convinced her.

'He was fine. Seriously. Not scary at all.'

'Of course you don't think he's scary,' she rolled her eyes. 'Girls like you would think he has that bad boy appeal.'

I took another sip and waited until the cold subsided. 'Girls like you?' I repeated. 'Define "girls like you".'

'Girls like you. Good girls who have a bit of an edge but are way too girl-next-door to do anything about it.'

My eyes widened. 'I nearly died in my caravan. I put an entire production into chaos. I was fired from my job. I've been to rehab and I'm living at home with my parents. I'm clearly not the girl-next-door!'

It was the first time I'd said those words to her, or to anyone. I didn't want pity. Maybe some empathy would have been nice. But instead, Sam looked me up and down and burst out laughing again. I laughed at her reaction.

When she caught her breath, she grabbed my hand. 'You got carried away, one time. You were a victim of a demanding job and a pretentious city. I did far worse things during my high school years than you will ever do in a lifetime. Things I would take back in an instant. I, my dear, am hardly the girl-next-door. I'm Angelina with a Billy-Bob tattoo and a vile of blood around my neck. And you're Angelina with little orphan kids and an ambassador for... well, whatever she's an ambassador for. You get what I'm saying.'

I took a drink and watched as Jack raised his fingers at Kate and she exchanged his empty glass with a full one.

Sam looked over her shoulder, then back at me. 'But I do want you to be careful. I can't stand seeing friends get hurt.'

I smiled half-heartedly. 'Can you get me a soda and lime? And maybe, if no-one's watching, add a tiny bit of Belvedere.'

She winked. 'One soda and water coming up. Then I better sort your brother out and make sure he knows what he's doing back there.'

I sat alone, sipping on my drink and watching Jack as he sat in silence. I felt my heart beat faster at the thought of talking to him, and when my vodka was gone, I mustered up the courage to sit beside him. Why does he make me so nervous?

His glass-focused gaze didn't break. He was almost done with his drink, so I asked for another scotch, which finally got his attention.

'You don't need to do that.' Between his quiet, low voice and the loud music, I could barely make out what he'd said.

'It's the least I could do.'

'How's the car?' He stared back at his drink and twisted the glass to make the scotch swirl inside.

'Apparently not worth fixing. Daughter-of-the-year right here.'

He either didn't hear me or didn't care. He raised his glass to his lips.

I intimidated most men who weren't in the same industry as me, but Jack wasn't the least bit interested in showing off, or wanting to know about who I worked with or how much money I had. It was a nice change.

'Bad day?' I asked, eluding to the scotch.

'Pretty ordinary,' he said. 'Who are you here with?'

'No-one,' I grinned. 'My friend owns the bar. I brought my brother in to get a job tonight. Now I'm drinking alone.'

He squinted, then looked away.

'Well, with you.'

'What?'

'I'm drinking with you.' I clinked my glass against his.

He tapped his glass. 'Looks like I'm the only one drinking.'

I asked the girl behind the bar for a straight vodka. If there were any paparazzi waiting, they would have had the money shot and Michelle would have had a heart attack. She expected me to lay low and behave. But I raised my glass to Jack and, despite Michelle's wishes, didn't take it off my lips until the last drop hit my tongue. It wasn't graceful. It certainly wasn't attractive. I've never been the type of girl to chug a drink, but I managed to do it without spilling any on my chin or shirt.

I sucked in my lips and looked to Jack. It was the first time I had seen a grin on his hardened face. I smiled back, flushed and dizzy.

'Where have you been hiding?' he muttered.

'I could ask you the same thing.'

He sipped the last few drops of his scotch and stared into his glass, contemplating another.

'Did you come from work?' I asked.

'Nope.'

'Were you meeting someone here?'

'Nope.'

'Just came in for a night cap?'

'Yup.' He turned to me, his grin gone. 'You ask a lot of questions.'

'It's a bit of a role reversal for me. I usually get asked the questions.'

He didn't respond.

'So, do you go out much?' I pressed.

'Not really.'

'I guess there's not many places to go in Rockford.'

'You don't have to do this.' He pushed his empty glass aside and straightened his shoulders.

'Do what?'

'Try to make small talk. I'm not angry at you for parking your car in the middle of the street.'

I smirked.

'It was an accident.' He stood, grabbed his wallet from his back pocket, pulled out a fifty dollar note and placed it under his glass. 'I've got your drink. Have a good night.'

He turned his back to me, and I spun around to watch him leave. 'Do you work tomorrow?'

'No,' he stopped and turned to me. 'I've got a day off. Why?'

'Well, you should check out the Dixon Races.' The words raced out of my mouth and I raised my folded hands to my chin. The Dixon Races were a Johns' family tradition for several years. Dad had shares in racehorses, so when I was young, we would all dress up, drive to Dixon and cheer along. Jimmy hated it, but I loved it. Not the racing so much, but the fashions, the excitement, the atmosphere and, as I got older, the betting.

'I'm not a gambling man.'

'Just a scotch-connoisseur?'

'Sure,' he put his finger in the air, as though he was giving a half-hearted salute. 'Bye, Ruby.'

Seven

A hurried, monotone voice echoed over the loud speakers and above the thunder of the racing horses. With a bet slip clasped in my hand, I tapped my toes and clenched my teeth. I had forgotten the thrill that came along with the anticipation of the races. A loud roar rose as the horses began their final stretch.

Except for Sam, I didn't know anyone in the crowd, and they didn't seem to recognise me under the fascinator netting draped over my new short hair. Either that or Sam was right – nobody cared.

Instead of wallowing in self-pity, I embraced the lack of attention, waved my arms and shouted arrogantly as the favourite took the lead, a nose ahead of my pick. As others celebrated their win, I scrunched my nose, then crumpled my losing bet slip and tossed it into the nearby bin.

'How much did you lose?' Sam asked. Her bright-green maxi dress and matching hat blended in with the women in bold colours who were trying not to spill their champagne as they navigated the grassy areas in their heels. Some had forfeited their shoes already and went barefoot.

'Ten,' I said while untwisting the strap of my dress. I thought by wearing black I would blend in. I was wrong.

'You're rich, and you're pissed you lost ten dollars?' She lifted her bet slip. 'I got her on the nose!! Should have one hundred big ones. I'm poor so I deserved this win more than you.'

'I'm not rich.'

'Not rich in your little world means drinking Chandon instead of Bollinger. I, my dear, am not rich, I mean, until now. I should do this betting thing professionally.'

I laughed. Some things never change. She had won an art contest in grade three and vowed to become the next Picasso. When she was eighteen and surprisingly passed her driver's licence with no deducted points – she decided she might become a professional driver: a limo driver, or stunt driver, or race car driver. When she discovered her love of beer, she decided to open a pub.

'I'm going to go collect my winnings, then head to work. I guess it's not exactly enough for me to quit just yet.' She leaned in and puckered her lips next to my cheek. 'Your brother's working tonight, Rubes. I told him he's my bitch.'

'Be nice.' I waved, and when her green frame vanished into the colourful crowd, I browsed through the hats and fascinators for anyone I may have known. My eyes fell on Dad.

I hadn't told him I was going to the races, as I'd expected him to be working. Mum said he rarely attended the meets since selling his horses. His three-piece navy suit and matching fedora were suitable for the races but not the law-firm. There was an unfamiliar woman with long, curly hair standing close to him. Tall and thin, she wore a red, skin-tight dress. She batted her eyelashes and threw her head back in laughter as Dad rubbed the small of her back and whispered in her ear. I froze, my blood running hot, a lump forming in my throat. I spun to leave but slipped, nearly falling as my head hit the shoulder of a man in a grey and white pinstriped suit and burgundy tie.

I straightened my fascinator and rubbed the tip of my nose before looking up to see Jack smiling down on me. I didn't realise how tall he was, until now. Even in heels, I barely reached his eyes.

'That's the second time we've crashed now, Ruby.'

My shoulders dropped and a grin swept over my face, despite my every effort to seem nonchalant. How was it that, when in front of a camera or audience, I could act my way through anything, but when in front of Jack, my body was stronger than my brain. 'Hey you.' I tried to sound calm despite my thumping heart. 'I thought you don't gamble?'

'I don't.' He leaned over the track fence, then looked back over his shoulder towards me. I stood beside him, rested my elbows next to his and studied his face. There was a short layer of hair on his scalp and stubble along his jaw, as if he hadn't shaved in a day or two. He had thick, dark eyelashes – the type many girls would pay top dollar for – and a few, soft freckles over his nose. He looked at me and I glanced away to the empty track.

'So you just came to watch?' I said.

'I guess I need to get out more.' His closed mouth drew up in the corners. 'You told me I should come, so... I'm here.'

'So...' I looked back to him. 'You're here.'

'Do you bet?'

'Yeah. It adds some excitement to it all.'

He sniffed. 'You find it more exciting when you stand to lose something?'

'I guess that's one way of looking at it. Or I find it more exciting when I can win.'

He shuffled closer, the heat of his mouth against my cheek. There was no scent of scotch. 'So I should take a chance?'

'Yes! You'll have more fun if you just take a chance, trust me. Win or lose.' I grabbed his hand and pulled him towards the bookies. He followed but jerked his hand back and slid it into his pocket. I blushed, but before I could apologise, he stepped further ahead and stopped at the growing line of waiting punters.

'Which one should I pick?'

'Well, you can go through their forms, the stats, etc. etc.,' I said. 'Or you can do what I do and choose by the name.'

'Alright.' He smirked. 'I'll put fifty dollars on Jumping Jack. It's only fitting, right?'

'Fifty! It's paying ten to one so that would be a good pay out if it gets up.' I looked into my race book, mostly because I was still hot with shame.

'What about you? What are you going to pick?'

'Hmmm.' I patted my book against my hip and looked at the list of names behind the bookies. 'I like NewYorkMiss. Only fitting, right?'

He squinted as he tilted his head in confusion.

I didn't explain. 'I'll match you – fifty dollars on the nose.'

As we walked back to the fence line, I looked for Dad and the mysterious woman, but they were gone.

'Looking for someone?' Jack asked.

I shook my head. 'No-one important.' We stopped, our elbows skimming. 'So, when did you get here?'

'Just as you ran into me,' he flashed me one of his slanted smiles. 'Literally.'

'Literally,' I repeated under my breath.

'I ended up getting called into work this morning and had just knocked off.'

'So you go to work in a suit?'

His smile didn't break. 'Just something I had in the closet.'

A PLAN UNRAVELLED

I nodded slowly. 'It looks nice on you.'

He rocked from his toes to his heels and looked forward. 'Or I may have ducked into a shop after work and made a quick purchase.'

I smiled, but before I could commend Jack on the effort he made to come to the races, a voice crackled over the speakers. The grandstands, which were empty a few minutes' prior, were now at capacity.

'You ready?'

Jack nodded, his face steady as the horses left the barriers. I watched him, his eyes, his lips. He remained calm as everyone around us yelled. Hooves rumbled down the track, grown men shouted and women screamed, but Jack remained firm. His head turned to follow the horses as they sprinted past. He raised his eyebrows and parted his lips, and when the horses crossed the finish line, he threw his fists in the air.

'You beauty!'

'Jumping Jack for the win!' The commentator shouted.

I yelped like a child. 'Oh-my-gosh, you won!'

'What are the chances?' He burst with laughter.

'What did I say?' I gently elbowed his ribs. 'Sometimes it pays to take a chance.'

'You were right.' He held up his ticket. 'This is the money ticket, right here!'

I tried to snatch it from his fingers, but he pulled it back. 'I don't think so.'

'Hmmm. You're not one of those sharks, are you? Like in pool? You pretend you have no clue, then start taking bets from others and make a small fortune?'

'Is that what you take me for?'

'I'm not sure. I haven't figured you out.'

He looked around to study the dispersing crowd. 'I don't have me figured out yet.'

I said, 'You're a pretty private person, hey?'

He didn't reply.

'Exactly my point.'

We made our way towards the bookies. As his elbow grazed mine, I became instantly aware of the chipped nail polish on the index finger of my left hand, and the scuff mark on my clutch. I brushed at it with my thumb, but it wouldn't budge. I don't know why I was worried about these imperfections; Jack didn't seem to take any notice at all.

Most men I'd met who weren't in the industry didn't care whether my hair was out of place or if I had lipstick on my teeth. They only wanted a night with me to gain bragging rights. But those men only knew Anna. Jack didn't know her at all. He didn't ask me about my past. Yet, for reasons I couldn't figure, I wanted to ask him everything about his.

We collected his winnings and he held out five crisp fifty-dollar notes.

'What's this for?'

'It's your half of the winnings.'

I pushed his hand back. 'No, you won it. It's yours.'

He tucked the money into his torn leather wallet as we walked past the food trucks, with the smell of pizza, popcorn and deep-fried chicken momentarily taking me back to New York. It was almost five o'clock and I'd been so fixated on placing bets with Sam that I hadn't eaten since breakfast.

'Why don't you buy me some fish and chips instead, and we will call it even?'

'Fish and chips?' he asked.

'You don't like fish and chips?'

He lifted his shoulders and tucked his hands in his pockets. 'I do, but I didn't take you as a fish and chips kinda girl.'

'What kinda girl do you take me for?'

He turned to me with one eye closed. 'I haven't figured you out just yet.'

'Well, I'll give you a hint. I'm usually a champagne and oyster girl. Most of the time, I'm a salad and water kinda girl. Not by choice,' I said. 'But lately I'm a vodka girl, and today I'm a fish and chips kinda girl.'

'Ah, so you're one of those.'

'One of what?'

'One of those "you never know what kinda girl you're gonna get" girls.'

I guided him to the fish and chips van. 'I guess so. Just like you, I'm still trying to figure myself out.'

'Well, that's one thing we have in common.'

We sat on the grass near the main stage, tearing the fish into pieces, dunking the chips in tomato sauce and being careful not to drip on ourselves. As we ate, we laughed at how horrid the band was, made fun of each of the drunken dancers and took turns trying to guess what each of them did as a living. By the time we reached the last chip, making a mess was the last thing on our minds.

'See her?' He slyly pointed at a woman dressed in white with wine stains on her chest and grass stains on her bum, flinging her arms and dancing in circles. Her eyes were tightly closed and her fascinator clung loosely to her curled hair. 'I think she's a mother of six.'

I giggled.

'She demanded of her husband that she gets one day out with her friends while he stays home with the crew. She's overindulged, rolled in the grass, and is now meditating while dancing, taking in her final moments before she gets back to real life: screaming kids; dirty nappies; spilled milk; endless laundry; Lego pieces hidden in the carpet, which jab her foot in the middle of the night when she's up for late feeds; and a lazy husband who leaves his dishes on the bench instead of putting them in the sink like she bloody asked him a million times before.'

'That's good. You did well.' I smiled. 'Do you have six kids at home?'

'Ha, no way in hell,' he said. 'Listening to some of the men at work, I think I've pieced together the horror that is family life.'

'The horror.' I smiled again before picking out two teenagers dancing close, swaying their bodies passionately and whispering into each other's ears. 'Those two there.'

'The tweens?'

'Yes, the tweens. They've been gushing over one another for a while now. Today they came with mutual friends. They all snuck vodka into water bottles and packed them in their picnic baskets. These two didn't talk to each other for the first five races, but after the vodka kicked in, she started making flirty eyes at him, and he stole any chance he could to sit or stand next to her.'

'Is that right?'

I nodded confidently. 'He waited until no-one was around to tell her she looked nice. She blushed. The races have ended and now he's telling her that he's been pining over her for years. It's really only been months, but at their age, months seem like years.'

'That's cute. But the real question is, is he getting lucky tonight?'

I looked her up and down. She was wearing a modest floral dress and little make-up. She opted for a white bow in her hair instead of the traditional race headwear. 'I don't think so. She'll make him wait.'

Jack shook his head slowly and clicked his tongue three times. 'Poor guy.'

I laughed. 'They're too young to throw themselves away.'

'Nah, they're allowed to have fun without falling in love.'

We had come up with stories for almost every dancing race-goer when the band played its final song and the last bus departed. I wished that time would freeze and I could sit with Jack for hours instead of returning to my parents and facing my deceiving father and naive mother.

When I was younger, I would struggle to look at Dad if I suspected a late-night tryst. Mum would kiss him, hand over a glass of wine and ignore the lingering perfume and the trace of shimmering bronzer that dusted the collar of his black suit. I dreamt of the day I could stare into his eyes and, without saying a word, have him feel the intense heat of my rage, which sweltered in every crevice of my mind and every inch of my soul. I wanted to unleash the fire, have him burn with shame. Instead, like a coward, I would turn a cheek or retreat to my bedroom, where I rehearsed lines until I fell asleep with my head buried in a script.

This time, there was no script to read or lines to learn. Jack was my only escape.

'Did you drive out here? Or have you handed in your licence?'

'You're a bit of smart arse, aren't you?'

'Nah. Just curious.' He had a faint dimple, which appeared when he smirked and softened his face.

'Well, I'll have you know I have a pretty good driving record. Well, I did. But then again, I never drove much until I moved back to Rockford. But to answer your question, I caught a ride, but my ride's left. I'll probably catch a cab.'

'There's not too many of those around here.' Jack spun his head to me. 'Have you forgotten where you are?'

I looked to the line of vehicles in the distance, waiting to leave the carpark. 'I guess, for a moment, I did.'

'I'll give you a ride back.'

I picked up my clutch and dusted the loose strands of grass from it. The scuff mark looked faint. Jack stood and held out his hand. It was warm, a little damp, and swallowed my fingers as I tried, but failed, to elegantly clasp my knees closed and keep my heels from sinking into the ground as I stood.

'You should just do what half the girls here have done and ditch the heels,' Jack suggested, pulling his hand back and tucking it in his pocket.

'I don't think I've had enough to drink to warrant going bare foot,' I said, slowly removing each shoe. 'But I guess if all the locals do it, I can do it too.'

'That'a girl.' Jack took the shoes from me and held them as we walked. 'So, where did you come from?'

I was surprised at his sudden interest, and it might have shown by the few seconds it took me to answer.

'You said something about not driving before you moved to Rockford?'

'I used to be a local. I grew up here several years ago,' I said. 'I moved to New York when I was seventeen, then came back about two weeks ago to stay with my parents for a few months – to give myself some timeout.' I expected some follow-up questions, but there were none.

'NewYorkMiss makes more sense now,' he said.

'What about you? Why did you move here, to Rockford?'

'Why not?'

I could have thought of several reasons – it was small, quiet, isolated. During my morning runs, I've noticed that the town still lacked any arts and culture, unless you counted the gallery in the main hall of the council building, which showcased different local exhibitors every week. Mum said that in the last few years a drama program had begun at the school, an art therapy class started for the sick at the Dixon hospital, and an annual talent quest had become a main feature at the annual Rockford Show. She said the winner won a meat tray, a bouquet of flowers and a grocery voucher.

There were a handful of clothing shops, a couple of antique stores and a few cafes. Everyone knew everyone's business, but nobody cared; however, it gave them something to talk about. My family name, for several years, rolled off the tongues of Rockford locals as they sipped coffee with their friends or stopped for a chat with their neighbour while collecting the mail. My father's promiscuity, my mother's ignorance, my success, my brother's failures.

I developed thick skin quickly. I didn't know it at the time, but the gossip prepped me for the tabloids – the headlines about my shrinking weight or a bad review. I handled it all with grace, Michelle would tell me. I didn't cop much bad press, though. The worst headline, before the scandal, was the gaudy dress I'd worn to my first red carpet event – an embarrassing ordeal. Coming from Rockford, I hadn't been fashion savvy. Michelle promptly hired a stylist.

'So, you work at the mines? What else do you do?'

'Not a hell of a lot. Work, eat, sleep, continue.' He stopped at the passenger side of his ute.

'What have you been doing here?'

'Mmm, I eat, sleep, continue,' I said. 'I've been going for runs, doing yoga and gardening. It's been exhilarating, really.'

The setting sun was hidden behind grey clouds and the few light poles scattered through the carpark cast a faint glow in the darkness. A soft breeze set in and a slight chill swept over my bare legs. I crossed my arms and rubbed my hands on my biceps, trying to produce some heat. Jack stripped off his jacket and moved closer to me, his warm breath falling faintly on my cold cheek, sending a hot rush through the rest of my body. His piercing gaze didn't falter as he leaned in and wrapped his jacket around my shoulders.

'A little summer breeze should be nothing compared to a New York winter,' he said. He opened the door for me, then circled his car keys around his index finger as he walked to his side.

We sat quietly, bumping along the narrow road towards Rockford.

'So no races tomorrow?' he asked, breaking the silence.

'Afraid not.'

'So just eating and sleeping on the agenda?'

'I guess so.' I stared at him, and when he noticed, he cast me one of his semi-grins that exposed his dimple.

I was hoping Jack would take a detour so that we could have driven around longer, but the day had to come to an end at some point. 'Thank you for the ride.' I held the door open.

'I'm going to have to start charging.'

'I'm in your debt.' I tried to sound more friendly than coy. 'So, see you around?'

'Yeah. I'll see you around.'

I walked towards the front door and heard the steadfast purr of his motor pull into the garage next door.

EIGHT

Jack had become a permanent fixture in my mind. I memorised his rugged and perfectly structured face – the wrinkles by his eyes, the stubble over his cheekbones and the way his lips parted slightly when he smirked. My mind replayed the sound of Jack's laugh and the husk of his voice.

I looked to his house in the mornings and throughout the days, hoping to catch a glimpse, but he was seldom there. He worked a lot, and when he came home, either retreated to his gym or to The Night Owl. I restrained myself from watching his workouts, but knew when they were in session from the glow of the light or, when we both had our windows open, the rumble of his music. Whether it was warm outside or windy and raining, I made sure to leave my window open.

I wanted to ask Sam more about Jack – what she'd heard from the other miners, what nights he went to The Night Owl for his scotch, what, if anything, there was that I needed to know. But after her initial warning, I decided against it.

Even over the phone, I could tell Sam was eating something. 'How did you... go after I left.... you at the races? Did you...' She coughed, then continued on between chews. 'Did you back a winner on the last?'

I was sprawled out on the couch flicking through channels with one hand, while holding my mobile against my ear with the other. Mum was in the kitchen, trying to mask her eavesdropping by vigorously stirring a cake batter. 'No good. You win some you lose some.'

'Oh, I should have stayed. Seems I was good luck,' she said with a mouthful. 'How was the bus home? Did the Dixon peasants realise there was royalty in their presence?'

'Ha, ha, ha. Good one,' I said playfully, dodging the answer.

'Jimmy did good last night.'

'Did he?' I tried to sound interested while finding something worthy of watching on television.

'Yeah. He showed up on time – overloaded with cologne to mask the smell of weed – but on time and smelling somewhat nice, nonetheless. He kept to himself, but did well.'

'That's good,' I split my attention between her and the television.

'Are you listening to me?'

A PLAN UNRAVELLED

'Yeah. On time, drenched in cologne, blah blah blah.' I straightened my back against the couch. 'Glad to hear he's working out for you. We all know he needs some kind of genuine income. He needs to get himself his own place. What are you eating?'

'A sandwich. Tuna. With potato chips and pickles.' She took a moment to swallow. 'Besides, isn't this a case of the pot calling the kettle black?'

'True. This, however, is temporary for me. And pickles? Anyone would have guessed you came from New York. That or you're knocked up.

'I've always liked pickles. Anyhoo, the reason I called was to see if you have plans tomorrow night.'

'Plans. Are you kidding me? If by plans you mean watching Netflix and chilling- which in my world means washing and drying my hair- then yes, I am very busy.'

'Washing and drying hair is a massive effort, so you'd be excused if that really was your plan. But since I am guessing you're lying to me, I have some real plans for you.'

I hummed deeply and bit my lip. 'What are they?'

'Sound a tad more excited!' she squealed.

I crossed my legs and tucked my slipper clad feet under my bum. 'Hmmm.'

'I've planned us a double date,' she said.

'Nooo, Sam.' I cringed. Mum peeked around the kitchen door, then back again. 'I am really not interested.'

'Oh, please, babe. You'll be doing it for me.'

'Why do you need me to go?'

'Well, you haven't met my boyfriend yet and I really want you and him to get along. And he's bringing a friend.'

'Sounds like a set up to me.'

'Please just come,' she pleaded. 'Besides, you need to swap your leggings and jumpers for something nice. And maybe run a brush through your hair. You're getting a little too comfortable here, if you know what I mean?'

'Hey now!' I screeched as I looked down at my oversized knit, black trackies and slipped clad feet. Maybe Sam was right. I was relaxed when it came to what I wore at home, and had given up on wearing make-up or perfecting my hair. But there hadn't been one lurking pap since I had returned to Rockford, and, besides the young girl at the market, there hadn't been much fanfare either. There was no-one to impress. Besides Jack.

'You need a good night out. Maybe you'll even get lucky.'

'Sam!'

'Don't tell me you don't want it. I'm sure you weren't scoring any at the mental institution, right? And unless you aren't telling me something, you certainly aren't getting any in Rockford.'

'It was a hospital. And I don't want any,' I whispered loudly, just as I did when I was a teenager hoping my mother wouldn't catch on to our conversations.

'Just don't be a poor sport and come along. You don't have to go home with the guy if you don't want. Just have some fun. Take a chance. Live a little!'

Ugh! Sam wasn't going to budge. 'Okay.'

'Oh, thank goodness.' She sighed in relief. 'Okay, so I said we would meet him at Alberto's. I'll pick you up.'

Alberto's was a tiny seafood restaurant that had been a staple in Rockford since I was a toddler. It was always booked out on weekends because the service and food equalled any chef-hatted city restaurant. It was fine-dining — too fancy for many of the middle-class Rockford residents. But somehow, after thirty years, it was still a town favourite.

'You got a table?'

'We did. I may have dropped your name but insisted no cameras or fanfare or anything,' she said. 'I can't wait!'

I rolled my eyes. 'I thought you said no-one in Rockford cares about celebrity status.'

'I was pinching at straws. It worked. I doubt anyone will give you a second glance.'

'I don't know how that's supposed to make me feel.' I sighed. 'But anyway, tell me, have you met my date before?'

'Uh, maybe...'

I sensed her tone, took a deep breath and asked again. 'Sammmm? What aren't you telling me?'

'Alright, it's Lucas.'

I nearly dropped my phone. 'Lucas, as in Lucas Rogers?'

Her voice went quiet and squeaky. 'Yesss.'

I dropped the remote and buried my face in my hands, body tense, heart racing. For a moment, I stopped breathing.

I had thought about Lucas often, but I didn't expect him to still live in Rockford, or to be single. Last I had heard, he had planned to move to Melbourne and, like my father, become a lawyer. That's why Dad was keen on him. Lucas was the son he never had. He had the passion and drive that Jimmy lacked, he was equally charming and masculine, he had style, grace and was confident. Dad loved confidence. So when Lucas and I broke up, Dad took it hard. He told me I would never find another man like Lucas. And, for once, I agreed. But I had dreams to chase, so something had to give.

Lucas was the only person who knew me intimately before there was New York, and a stage name, and money and fame. He, for a large part, was responsible for my success. He studied lines with me for school plays, though I knew it pained him to do so. When I wanted to sneak out to parties with Sam, he was the responsible voice in my head reminding me of the plan I wrote when I was eight years old. He was the one who pinned it on my desk in hopes it would motivate me. Lucas was, I thought, my biggest fan. Though Mum would probably contest the title until she was blue in the face.

Lucas, of course, had his own plans and worked hard to achieve them. He was smart. Not just top-of-the-class, bookworm smart. He was street smart. He was family-orientated. He was an only child but loved my family like his own. After school, when he wasn't with me, he took care of his ailing mother until she succumbed to her early onset of Alzheimer's, when he was in Year 11. He then became the rock for his severely depressed Dad. With all the pain Lucas had harboured, not once did I see a single tear drop from his big dark eyes. He was a sensitive soul, wrapped in a thin, five-foot-ten build, which to the untrained eye would be easy to snap. But those who were close to him knew he was guarded by an invisible concrete shield even the largest sledgehammer would struggle to crack.

And even while studying for exams, applying for law school, dealing with the death of his mother and helping his father through his grief, Lucas still made me feel as if I were the only person in his life. I tried to be there for him, but he insisted he was okay, that he would be fine. It was with this wall he built, and the love he gave, that he insisted I leave him and pursue acting in New York.

'You're destined to be a star,' he said as he kissed me goodbye at the airport. 'You already are.'

We broke things off. We knew long-distance would be too hard. He wrote me a few emails after I left and sent me a few photos, and I did the same. But life got busy, our priorities changed and we stopped talking.

'You have to be kidding me. Lucas?' I asked again, knowing the answer hadn't changed.

'Are you mad?'

'I didn't expect to see him. I didn't know he still lived here.' My stomach churned and my toes tapped. 'Does he know I'm only back for three months?'

'He knows you're back for a short break. I told him. He's just looking forward to seeing you and catching up.' Her voice rose again. 'Give it a chance.'

I took a deep breath and steadied my toes. 'Okay. Okay, but easy on us hooking up, alright?'

'Yeah, yeah. It's just like old times,' she laughed. 'I'll pick you up at seven.'

NINE

I stared blankly into my reflection and struggled to recognise the blonde woman looking back. My black leather pants hugged my waist a little tighter than they did in New York, my skin was darker, my cheeks seemed rounder. My damn toe was tapping again.

I rummaged through my make-up case which, apart from the race day, I'd barely opened. I changed my earrings several times, but when I heard a car pull into the driveway, I quickly put my earring back in my jewellery box and pulled out a vintage ruby and diamond ring. I'd bought it shortly after my first big pay check, but I stopped wearing it religiously after about a year or so. If Michelle knew I had an expensive, rare ring in my possession, I'm sure she'd make me hawk it. The thought had crossed my mind, especially when I looked at my dwindling bank account, but I could never bring myself to sell it.

I slid it on my finger and glanced to the window. Jack's ute wasn't in his driveway.

Though I'd been anxious about seeing my first love again, I'd managed to keep my nerves at bay by thinking about Jack. I now peeked out the window every morning, or before I tucked into bed. When he came home from work, then left again shortly after, I assumed it was to The Night Owl. I'd been searching for an excuse to return to the pub and see him again, but I didn't have the courage. My mind was bouncing between two men. One who stole my heart many years ago, who knew all my habits, my dreams and my fears and who so easily deciphered the gaze from my eyes or tone of my voice. And one who I knew nothing about, but whose mystery was strangely enthralling and whose oblivion was surprisingly refreshing.

'Going somewhere?' Jimmy muttered from my bedroom door.

I looked in the mirror and teased the roots of my hair with my fingers. 'I am. Aren't you working tonight?' I hoped he wouldn't pry further.

'I am, in half an hour. Who are you going out with?'

'Sam, her boyfriend and another friend.'

Jimmy scrunched his forehead. 'A friend?' He moved to my bedroom window at the sound of the car horn, and I grabbed my leather jacket and swung it on.

'Lucas.' I shot him a look. 'If you must know.'

'Lucas? Like the Lucas?'

'Don't make a fuss over it. It's just a catch up.'

He crossed his arms and bit his pursed lips. 'Okay. But judging on your appearance you're making a big fuss over it.'

'I didn't think it was appropriate to go for dinner in Uggs and sweats.'

'They're called trackies. You're in Australia now.' He leaned against the doorframe and crossed one ankle over the other. 'I'm glad you're getting out and about. I hate seeing you moping around here.'

The horn sounded again. 'I've been getting out.'

'Where?'

'I went to the market. And to the races.'

'Yeah, but that's it.'

He was right, but the two outings in Rockford were a lot less stressful than the events I'd attended in New York over the past twelve months. Michelle tried to secure me invites to every party, awards evening and Premiere on offer. I would have attended the opening of a can of soup if possible. I wasn't considered elite enough for several occasions, but for the events I did attend, I felt enormous pressure to look outstanding so that I was noticed by anyone important. Michelle also insisted I self-promote and rub shoulders with people who could help further my career. It was work. It wasn't a social life.

'Bye, Jimmy.' I smirked as I walked past him.

'Good luck. Have fun. Tell Lucas I say hi.'

'Maybe we'll stop by later for a drink,' I yelled over my shoulder.

'Righty-o,' he muttered back.

My heels clunked against the stairs as I scurried towards the door. Mum sat at the kitchen table with a cup of hot tea at arm's length. She peered up from her laptop. 'You look nice.'

'Thank you. Don't wait up.' I wasn't about to disclose any information that wasn't requested. I closed the door behind me and got into Sam's car.

Her hair was down and curled, pink lipstick stained her lips and part of her teeth, and she smelled as though she had emptied a bottle of cheap perfume on her neck.

I pressed my finger against my teeth prompting Sam to run her tongue along hers.

'Good?' she asked with clenched teeth.

'All good.'

She whistled as we drove to the restaurant. I stared out the window, my fingers shaking against my legs and my toes tapping against the floor mat.

'Calm down, Twiggy.' Sam rested her hand against my leg. 'Deep breath. Steady feet. Keep reminding yourself of that. Everything will be okay.'

'It's just weird, you know?'

'Not really.'

'It's been so long. So much has changed.'

'Then you'll have a lot to talk about. No awkward silences.'

She continued to whistle and rocked her head back and forth to the radio as we drove, her hand making rolling waves out the window. I admired her contentment. A stark contrast to the neurotic, highly strung girl I had once known, yet, with the same zest for life.

She put her window up as we parked in the narrow carpark outside Alberto's. The building was originally a school house, during early settlement, and had been converted to a café before the owners of Alberto's purchased it and transformed it once again. The original brickwork was retained, but the wrap-around oak veranda was a new addition. Dimly lit patio lanterns hung from the ceiling, setting the ambience. As we approached the entrance, Sam sensed my nerves and put her hand between my shoulder blades and softly rubbed, just like my mother used to do when I was a child lying in bed crying because I'd had a nightmare or I was missing Dad.

A buzz of whispers and a swarm of eyes stung me as we entered. I straightened my back and smiled politely while Sam gently pushed me through the narrow aisles between the tables. She had already spotted her boyfriend and Lucas sitting at a table at the back.

'You okay?' Sam whispered.

It was the most public attention I'd received since arriving in Rockford. I'd desperately wanted to be noticed in the Big Apple, and I relished the attention I was given, but over the past few weeks, I felt relieved of the pressure to look a specific way – no-one would expect me to be composed and elegant while picking up toilet paper in the supermarket, or to powder my red nose, or cough into a pretty hanky when I was battling a cold. Maybe I was now oblivious to such attention – while I was in fitness mode during my morning runs, or when I was fixated on Jack in the dark, loud pub. But in the small, confined space of Alberto's, about to come face-to-face with my high school sweetheart, I was reminded of the girl I had once been.

'I'm fine,' I lied.

'Good,' she whispered back, though we both knew I was lying.

We approached the small table in a back corner of the restaurant and my chest felt heavy as I caught Lucas's gaze.

He looked like a musclier, aged version of his former self. His signature, black curly hair still fell loosely over his face. His dark brown eyes were still wide under his thick bushy eyebrows. The lower half of his face was darkened, like he had only recently shaved off a thick beard, adding a masculine trait he hadn't sported when I'd dated him. His fitted collared shirt showed that his bony arms had bulked up, his suit jacket over the back of his chair showed he had grown a sophisticated style, and a Rolex on his wrist was a trophy of his success.

Sam's boyfriend sat next to Lucas. He had a short scruffy beard and sun-faded hair pulled into a messy man bun. He wore a blue jumper over a white shirt and dark brown cuffed pants that came inches short of his ankles showing off his bright blue suede loafers.

Lucas stood and wrapped his arms around me so tightly I couldn't tell the difference between my beating heart and his.

'It's good to see you, Rubes. It's been too long.'

'It has, hasn't it?' The tension from my shoulders lifted. 'Fifteen years?'

'Strange,' he said. 'It seems like longer, yet on the other hand, I feel like you never really left.'

I took a deep breath.

'You look amazing.'

'You do too,' I said, my heart slowing.

'Ruby, this is Harry.' Sam intertwined her arm in her boyfriend's.

I shook his hand and took a seat across the table from Lucas. The others followed.

'I'm a fan. Is that weird?' Harry slurred slightly, reminding me of Jimmy.

'I'm a fan of fans. And since you are Sam's lover, I am a fan of yours.' I shifted the serviette over my lap as they laughed. When I lifted my head, Lucas's lips were tight and his wistful eyes were set on me. I wondered what he was thinking. I wondered if he was proud of the person I had become or if he pitied me. Did he still think I was beautiful? Or had I become a mould of the typical American actress.

'I'm a fan too.' He smiled. 'Always have been.'

Within moments, a waiter arrived at our table and Harry ordered a bottle of red wine for us to share, then asked me if that was okay. I didn't know if he asked because he was unsure whether I should be drinking, given the scandal, or whether I didn't approve of his choice.

'That sounds great, Harry,' I reassured him.

It didn't take long before Lucas was telling stories of our past relationship and we were in hysterics remembering the finer times in our lives. The more we drank, the more we laughed. I could feel Lucas's eyes rest on me between stories. On one occasion, between jokes and sips, he winked at me like he did when we were younger, time and time again. He used to proudly point out how it would make blush.

This time, I couldn't tell if it was him, or just the sentimental feeling of a simpler time, that warmed my cheeks.

'You're blushing,' he said.

'Is it hot in here?' I asked playfully. 'So, where are you working now?' I changed the subject while sawing at my undercooked steak. Blood poured from the centre and over the top, soaking my buttered peas in red jus.

'James and Matthews. Dealing mostly with family law. Divorces, will disputes, custody, that sort of thing.'

'Wow, interesting.' I raised my eyebrows but remained focused on the dripping red meat stuck at the end of my fork. It had been so long since I sunk my teeth into a steak that I'd forgotten the texture of undercooked meat made me gag. I threw my hand over my mouth and forcefully swallowed.

'No, not really.' He chuckled, his elbow on the table and his fork in the air. 'It's terrible.'

I laughed at his honesty, dropping my fork to the table. 'No?'

'No. Not what I set out to do. But I was approached in law school and thought, why not. I'd like to do criminal law – like your old man.'

'You don't want to be like him.'

'Still up to his old ways?' He leaned back and sipped his wine.

'He won't change,' I said, picking up my fork again and eyeing it up.

'Well, that's a shame, Ruby. Some people don't know a good thing when it slaps them in the face.' He sat the glass down and picked into what little of his flounder he had left. 'I want to be like him when it comes to his career. He's good at what he does, he's respected in his profession.'

'Well, I'm guessing you aren't doing too bad yourself.'

'Coming from you, Miss Big Screen,' he smiled.

'Well, I can't take all the credit for that. I had a few people who backed me along the way.' I winked.

'We just cheered you on, you ran the race.' He finished chewing. 'You're not going to eat that, are you?'

'I asked for medium, didn't I?'

'You did. That's rare.' He pointed his finger. 'But you wouldn't have been satisfied with medium. You only ever ate it well-done.'

The fact Lucas had remembered – even if it was an insignificant detail about my meat preferences – drew a nostalgic tug at the corner of my lips.

That evening, I learned that Lucas and Harry had met in Melbourne. Lucas returned to Rockford six months ago, when his father died. The quiet streets and the slower pace enticed Lucas to stay. He found a job, bought a house. Harry, a bricklayer, followed. Harry set up his own business, bought a unit, and within a week of the move, met Sam.

Harry and Lucas told us stories of when they backpacked up the east coast, the home brew beer they made and got gravely ill from drinking, about the basketball games they played during their free time.

I offered to pay the bill – a move Michelle would have protested, given my latest bank statements – but Lucas and Harry insisted on picking up the tab. Lucas held the door open for us, and as we walked into the warm breeze, he wrapped his arm around me.

'So, should we keep this night going? Maybe go for a drink somewhere?' Harry asked. Until then, I hadn't thought of Jack all night, but when Lucas suggested we head to The Night Owl, I felt that familiar knot in my stomach.

A PLAN UNRAVELLED

'No! I'm there every day,' Sam groaned. 'Let's go to yours, Lucas.'

We squashed four of us into Harry's three-seater ute. Luckily the drive was only a few minutes, and we arrived at a one-story, blue rendered house.

I followed them inside, took off my shoes and moved through the entrance and down the hall, admiring the beauty of every decorative piece along the way. There was a porcelain dish on the front marble entrance table, a vibrant abstract painting on the wall and a woollen floor runner in the same blues and yellows over the wooden floor. The rug was so beautiful that I didn't want to step on it, but Lucas did, so I followed.

We walked into the spacious living room. Lucas decided against turning on the lights and instead started the gas fire. Not one piece of furniture looked out of place among the dark floor and grey walls. The black coffee table matched the sideboard, the brown leather couch was accessorised with black cowhide cushions. I wondered whether he'd decorated the house or a stylish woman in his life had given him some tips.

'I'll get us some more wine,' Lucas said, heading to the adjoining kitchen.

Sam and Harry cuddled on the couch and turned on the television. I slowly walked around the room, studying photos of Lucas's parents, a familiar restored grandfather clock, which stood next to a closed, brown leather box adorned with the skull of a bull, or a ram, or some animal with large horns. I stopped at a glass-cased bookshelf and studied the contents – numerous law textbooks, a variety of popular classical literature from Charles Dickens to William Shakespeare to George Orwell and the Bronte sisters. I ran my fingers across the row of Superman comics on the bottom three shelves and recalled Lucas's childhood hobby, which lingered into his teens and, evidently, into his adulthood. My mouth parted as I thought back to the countless times he would drag me into old bookstores and antique shops, looking for something to add to his prized collection. I'd stand behind him, embarrassed, as he asked the shop owners for help, or get stuck into a deep conversation about action heroes and special editions. It was this one desire of his that I never understood, nor could share an interest in. It was a quirky characteristic which threw shade on his usually dignified and practical poise.

'Impressed by my comics?' Lucas stood behind me and handed me a glass of red wine.

'I thought you might have given up.'

'Nah. I know when to let things go and when to keep going.'

'Of all things to pursue.' I grinned.

'Yeah.' he leaned up against the bookshelf to face me. 'There's something missing. I don't feel complete just yet.'

I took a small sip of wine and, almost afraid to ask, muttered, 'What's that?'

He turned to the bookshelf and pointed at the books. 'Number seven. If I find it, I will complete volume one of the Action Comics series.'

I took a big swig, swished it around in my mouth and nodded as I swallowed. 'Right.'

'December 1938. *Superman Joins the Circus*. He was on the cover.'

'I remember you telling me that all those years ago.'

'And I am still hunting that one book down. Worth an absolute fortune,' He looked around the room then back at me. 'Lame, maybe, but I'm not giving up.'

'Good,' I said, elbowing him. 'Don't give up. But I doubt you'll find what you're looking for in Rockford.' I sat on the floor, next to the fire, away from Sam and Harry who were deep in conversation. Lucas sat beside me, crossed his legs and rested back on an elbow.

'You never know. Rockford is full of surprises.' He looked at me. 'I didn't find what I was looking for in Melbourne.'

'Melbourne.' I sighed. 'Why do I have the feeling you aren't just talking about comic books?'

'Because I'm not,' he said. 'There wasn't much of anything for me there. I wasn't satisfied being away from Dad, work was ordinary, love was non-existent.'

'Oh, I don't believe that,' I said playfully.

'What? What part?'

'The love part,' I said. 'How could you have trouble in love?'

He let out an exaggerated groan and stretched his back, resting his hands on the floor to prop himself up. 'I was married, Ruby.'

My mouth sprung open. 'Oh. I didn't know. I mean, I'm not surprised that you were married.'

'It was stupid, really,' he said. 'We met at law school, quickly fell in love, went on a trip to Hawaii and spontaneously eloped. It was out of character for the both of us, and I think that's why we did it. We both felt like we were on the straight and narrow, life was mundane, and we wanted to do something wild.'

'I get that.'

'We thought we knew what we were doing, that it all made sense. But we got back to Melbourne, settled back into our house, worked long hours, argued a lot, and just as quickly as I had fallen in love, I fell out of it.' He took a sip of his wine and looked ahead. 'I felt sick to my stomach about it all. Then one day, she came home and told me she didn't love me and wanted a divorce. She expected me to cry, or beg and plead, or whatever, but I think I gave her a big hug and kiss and told her I felt the same way.'

'What?' I shrieked in disbelief.

'I know, crazy, right?' He looked back to me. 'She was relieved that I was relieved and we spoke about it for a bit, came up with a plan that evening and booked into our favourite restaurant to celebrate. She packed her bags the next day, we shook hands, and haven't spoken since.'

I didn't hide my shock. 'Wow.'

'I know, strange, right?'

'I wasn't expecting that. Not from you.'

'I guess we both have done things a little out of character.'

Until then, Lucas hadn't alluded to the overdose. Now, the statement felt like a blow.

'With everything that happened, are you going to go back to New York, or will you stay in Australia?'

I ran my finger around the top of my glass, searching for the right words. 'Yeah, I mean, this is only temporary.'

He waited for me to elaborate, but I bit my lip.

'But you don't want New York to eat you alive,' he said.

I stayed silent. How could he understand the complexity of what I had been though?

'Think about what it did to you.' He paused with a look of regret for saying too much.

I put my hand on his knee. 'It's okay.'

He shuffled a bit closer and I took my hand away.

'So, what is next for you?'

'I'll go back. I need to go back. My life is there. My dreams are there. I just need a little break. No scripts, no cameras, no headlines.'

'You could do anything you wanted to in Australia, you know? You did New York. You went and conquered.'

'Not quite.' I laughed under my breath.

'You did pretty well, Ruby. And I think your time there came to an end for a reason. You can now come back and do whatever you want to do here. You were always a motivated girl, and after talking to you tonight, I think you're the same girl you were fifteen years ago.'

His eyes steadied on mine, and I didn't know whether to look away or accept his advances. If I kissed him, I ran the risk of landing myself in the same position I'd faced fifteen years prior. He was hard to leave and hard to get over.

As Lucas leaned in, I turned and bowed my head. I felt him do the same. His forehead rested against my cheek.

'I'm sorry,' he whispered.

'No, I am. I'm just...'

'You don't have to explain yourself.'

'I don't want to dig up...'

'Hey, I said you don't have to explain yourself.'

We stared at each other for seconds before I raised my shoulders and lifted myself up off the ground. 'I should probably go.'

He stood. 'Okay, but can I call you? We can meet for a coffee or a walk or something. No strings attached?'

A PLAN UNRAVELLED

    I kissed him on the cheek, like I did to most of my friends. 'Of course.'

TEN

I wiped Nutella from the corner of my mouth and wrapped my lips around my finger. Mum was three minutes into a spiel about the yoga retreat, but I was too heavily invested in my toast to take much notice. It had been years since I was able to indulge in such a treat, and until I found the container in the cupboard, I'd nearly forgotten Nutella existed.

'We will have to leave quite early,' she said, grabbing my crumb filled plate and stacking it into the dishwasher. 'I've told the ladies and they're glad you're coming along.'

I grabbed my orange juice and looked across the table to Dad, who rolled his eyes. I had avoided speaking to him much since the races.

'We'll drive up and meet the others there.'

Dad folded the newspaper and picked up his briefcase from under the table.

'I can't wait, Ruby. I think a weekend away is just what the doctor ordered. Life can get hectic, then it's too quiet, especially in Rockford. But I don't have to tell you that.' She closed the dishwasher and proceeded to wipe the benches. 'We need to breathe in the good and exhale the bad.'

Dad snickered.

'Now, now.' Mum turned and flashed him a look. 'What is with your attitude?'

'I highly doubt what your daughter wants is a weekend away with her mother and her friends who will probably pull their muscles or break a hip attempting to keep up with the rest of the young, limber yoga retreaters.' He closed the briefcase and walked to the front door.

Mum shook her head. 'How rude of you.'

'I'm a realist. It's about facts.' Dad put his hand on the door handle but froze when he peered out the front window. 'The neighbours have hired Ron?'

Ron was a gardener, hired by many of the Rockford locals who could afford him. He had been around since as long as I could remember. I was only a baby when Mum hired him off the back of recommendations, but within months of his employment, he and his wife Linda became close friends with Mum and Dad. I vaguely remember them laughing in our living room over drinks in the evening, having barbecues, travelling to Queensland together. Then, one day, it just stopped. As I got older, I questioned the breakdown, but Dad would shrug and Mum wouldn't answer.

I'd see them from time to time. Ron always gave a friendly wave, but Linda would turn her chin and stick up her nose. They'd left town when I was in high school, and guessing by Dad's surprise at the front door, had only just returned.

Mum gripped the kitchen bench. 'Ron? Ron Kingston?' She let out a small cough and wiped her cloth over the same spot on the bench several times. 'I haven't seen him in years.'

Dad cleared his throat. 'Ron Kingston. I can't believe he would be so vain as to show his face around here after all these years.' He opened the door and closed it gently as he left.

Mum grabbed her hot cup of tea, cradled it in her hands and walked to the front door. Her chest rose slowly as she looked out the window. 'He hasn't changed,' she murmured. Her eyes were fixated, her pout subtle. It was the same concentrated face I would see her pull during our yoga sessions. Her toes began to tap. Not the quick, anxious tapping I had annoyingly inherited from her, but a slow and controlled tap. Her head only shifted at the sound of Jimmy on the stairs.

He had a peculiar way of descending – one foot on a step, then the other meeting up. His scruffy hair was covered by the black hood on his unzipped jumper. A wrinkled t-shirt peeked through. He passed Mum and me and made himself a cup of coffee.

I wrinkled my nose at the mixed smell of body odour and weed.

'I think you need to wash your clothes,' I said. 'And since when do you drink coffee?'

Jimmy put his cup on the kitchen bench, lifted his shirt and sniffed. He shook his head as though he couldn't sense the stench.

'Since I started working late nights,' he said, before taking a sip of his coffee. 'Would you like to recommend something else to keep me awake?' He shot me the same sly look he'd given me as a kid. Mum had told me to never let my younger brother get under my skin, and following her advice, I learned to take Jimmy's remarks as nothing more than playful banter. Even if he was alluding to the scandal at New York.

'Get stuffed.' I flipped him the middle finger and squinted my eyes.

He chuckled while stirring the sugar, then sat next to me and turned to the sports pages of the newspaper. 'How was your date?'

Mum smiled suspiciously as she joined us at the table. 'I thought you were going on a date! Now, tell your mother who it was with.'

'Lucas,' Jimmy answered for me.

'Lucas!' Mum could hardly contain her excitement. 'Oh, Lucas! I always loved him. How is he doing now?'

'It wasn't serious,' I said. 'It was just two friends catching up.'

'Well, you should bring him around to the house.' She stood and put a piece of bread in the toaster while talking over her shoulder. 'I would love to see him. It's been so long. I didn't even know he was living in Rockford.' She stared out the small window looking towards the front yard.

'He moved back six months ago,' I said, before turning my attention back to Jimmy. 'Remember Ron, the gardener? He's back. He's working at the neighbours'.'

Mum spun her head to Jimmy, who returned her wide-eyed gaze.

'Ron Kingston?'

Mum sucked in her lips and nodded slowly.

'What's going on?' I asked.

Jimmy looked back at the newspaper and quickly flicked through the pages. 'Nothing's going on. I'm just surprised he's back. I haven't heard of him for a while.'

The toast popped up and Mum ran a knife over it several times with such pressure I was surprised she didn't tear a hole through it.

'Jumping Jack is racing today. It won me three hundred last week.' Jimmy seemed eager to change the subject and divert Mum's attention from the over-buttered toast. 'I better put a bet on.'

Mum placed the toast on a plate and set it in front of Jimmy. 'You shouldn't be betting. It's not good for your mental health, Jimmy. Can't people just enjoy the races without risking their hard-earned money? Why risk losing it all?'

A PLAN UNRAVELLED

Jack's face popped into my mind, albeit it wasn't the first time I'd thought of him that morning. I had woken to his ute pulling out of the driveway and peeked through the curtains in time to see the back tyre and tray disappear.

I excused myself from the table and headed to my room. Grabbing my phone off my bedside charger, I roamed though the names until I found Jack, just above Lucas.

I ran my thumb slowly over both names. A rush ran through my body and not wanting the adrenaline to go to waste, turned the screen off and grabbed my sneakers for a morning run.

Dripping in sweat and lost in music, I slowed my pace as I reached the front yard. I took out my earbuds and let them dangle over my shoulders. Mum had her back to me, chatting with Ron over the dividing white picket fence. Though she had shut down several times over the years whenever his or Linda's name was mentioned by her friends or acquaintances, Mum was never one for confrontation or grudges, so I wasn't surprised that she was being friendly. 'I'm my biggest ally, but friends and family are there for support,' she once said. 'Yet, I can be my worst enemy, so what's the point in making more?'

It was Dad who wasn't shy of speaking his mind or baring a cold shoulder.

'Well, look who's all grown up.' Ron held a whipper snipper in his dirt-stained gloves. He was wearing knee-length khaki shorts, a blue polo shirt and had a head full of silky silver hair, perfectly swept back. 'Ruby, or should I say, Anna Johns.'

With hands on my hips, I slowly walked over and stood beside Mum. 'Hi, Ron. How have you been?'

'I've been good. Good,' he said. 'And you? I've been following all your success. You make Rockford proud.'

'I doubt many are proud of me right now.' If he had followed my success, he would have been aware of my failures.

'Oh, don't worry about that, Ruby. Nobody is perfect. We all make mistakes.' He flashed a pitied look to Mum, then back to me. 'The only difference is that you've been in the public eye, so you can't hide your skeletons in the closet.'

'And to think I wanted so badly to be in the public eye.'

'Well, you've heard that adage, "be careful what you wish for".' He rubbed his hands together. 'Anyway, forget about it. You're home now, among people who will treat you like Ruby, not Anna.'

'Home. There's that word again,' I muttered before switching the topic. 'So, how's Linda?'

'She's good, yeah. Linda's good,' he said.

'Ron was in the middle of telling me how he and Linda travelled all over the world for a few years, then decided to move back to Rockford last month,' Mum said.

'We went to Europe and Asia. It was a trip of a lifetime. We lived, ate and drank like royalty. We saw every tourist attraction and tried everything on offer. We left no stone unturned.' He laughed. 'We decided to move back, and I didn't feel like sitting around doing nothing, so I thought I'd get back into gardening for casual work, and Linda volunteers at the op shop on Main Street. We need to keep ourselves busy. I learned a few tips and tricks from the magnificent gardens in...'

I suddenly remembered how much Ron could talk given the chance. My mind travelled, leaving his voice buried under my piling thoughts. It was nearly noon and Jumping Jack was about to race – an opportunity I couldn't waste. No matter how unchartered the territory was for me, no matter how daunting, I wanted so badly to see Jack again, and the winning stallion was the knock on my door.

'Well, it was good to see you again, Ron.'

He hadn't finished his sentence, but with each story dragging into another, I didn't have time to wait.

'Likewise.' He lifted a finger to say goodbye, then turned to Mum and continued from where he left off.

Holding onto my sudden braveness, I skipped up the stairs two at a time, picked up my phone and quickly pressed on Jack's name before I could convince myself otherwise.

My heart hadn't slowed much, but I couldn't tell if it was from the run or from the unanswered rings. I was about to hang up when I heard his quiet and uncertain voice.

'Uh, hello.'

'Jack?'

'Yeah?'

'Sorry,' I said, recognising he had no idea who was calling him. 'It's Ruby.'

Silence.

'Ruby Jones.' My confidence turned to embarrassment.

'I only know one Ruby.' He sounded cold and uninviting.

'Hey, so.' I scrambled for words. 'Um, This may sound odd, but my brother was going through the paper this morning and said Jumping Jack was racing again. I just thought I would give you a heads up in case you wanted to win another few hundred.' My nervous laugh resembled the sound of a toy machine gun.

'I don't like to gamble, remember?' I couldn't sense his tone beneath the noise of the heavy machinery rumbling behind him.

'Right, but you said that last time.' I was hoping he would engage in any kind of conversation, but there was nothing.

'Hey, sorry, I'm at work so I should get back to it.'

I threw my hand over the side of my scrunched face, rubbed my forehead and muttered, 'Okay.'

Rejection. It was my first year in New York when I was first stabbed with it. I stood in an audition room, with three casting directors whispering among themselves and letting out shallow laughs before showing me the door.

'I'm not cut out for this,' I told Michelle.

'Anna, some roles aren't made for you' she said. 'Know when to accept it and move on. Don't sulk. Get over yourself.'

ELEVEN

We were tucked away in a dark booth. Harry had his arm around Sam, and Lucas sat with his shoulder against mine, sipping on a glass of red. I was halfway through my second vodka and soda water when Jack walked into the pub. He took his usual seat at the bar and Kate poured him a scotch. I watched Jack as Jimmy collected empty beer glasses from a vacant table behind him.

Lucas caught me staring. 'So is Jimmy happy here?'

'Yeah, he is.' I turned my attention to Lucas. 'He needs to find something more though. He can't spend his life clearing tables.'

'Sure, he can. Nothing wrong with it,' Sam scolded. 'He gets a decent wage and socialises, a bit anyway. I'll tell you what he needs. He needs to be around people.'

'He's a grown man. He doesn't need anyone telling him what he needs,' Harry chimed in. 'Let him do what he wants.'

A PLAN UNRAVELLED

I looked at Jack again and watched as he took swig after swig of scotch. He looked into his glass, then, as though he felt my stare on his skin, turned to me. Embarrassed from my earlier phone call, I looked away quickly but returned to Jack's unwavering blue eyes. Sam, Harry and Lucas didn't notice the stare-off and continued to talk among themselves. I flashed a closed-mouth grin, but Jack's face didn't move until Lucas sprung his arm around my back and rubbed his hand on my shoulder.

Jack continued his drinking routine.

Harry whispered in Sam's ear and she scrunched up her face and giggled. Lucas looked at me and grinned at Harry and Sam's public display of affection and, at one point, took his hand from around my shoulder and placed it on my knee. I flinched, and he quickly took it off and tapped the table with his fingers.

I had accepted Lucas's offer of another group date, hoping I would have a nice evening out with old friends, but I worried about giving into the past and launching into a relationship that would again take me so long to get over. I'd spent years learning to channel the love we had, and the heartbreak I experienced, into my acting. Now, confronted with Lucas being back in Rockford at the same time as me, I wanted some clarity about my mixed feelings. The fact I had such quick reflexes and was so easily distracted provided some answers.

'So, maybe we can get together this week, for lunch or something?' Lucas looked at his watch. It was nearly midnight.

I took a deep breath.

'It's just lunch,' he smiled. 'We still have so much to catch up on and it would be nice to do so without all these other people around.' He tilted his head to Sam and Harry, who were nose to nose and nearly lip to lip.

'Okay,' I grinned.

'Okay. Great,' he mouthed back. 'Well. I've got to work tomorrow morning, so I should get going. Can I walk you home?'

'I might stick around and wait for Jimmy.' There was still an hour before he knocked off and I was buzzing from the vodka.

Lucas offered to wait, but I insisted I'd be fine. Harry and Sam left with him, and unfortunately, Jack followed suit.

'Drinking alone isn't a good look,' Jimmy said, clearing our empty glasses. He wiped the sticky residue on the table, surely built up over months. When the liquid mess wouldn't clear, he dropped the cloth on the tray of glasses and sat next to me.

I raised my glass. 'I'm drinking this because it looks like water. Water's not a bad look.'

'Strategic,' he said.

'Actually, I thought I'd finish this one and see if you wanted a walking buddy.'

'I've still got an hour left,' he said, leaning back against his seat and carefully studying my face. 'What's the real reason you didn't leave with Lucas?'

'That is the real reason.'

I flinched, knowing I wasn't getting off that easy with Jimmy. Like the director who once asked me, 'If you don't believe in your own act, how can you convince others?'

'No, it's not.' Jimmy rested his elbows on the wet, sticky table. 'Talk to me, sis.'

I glared at him the way I used to when he won Monopoly. He would raise his arms proclaiming victory, stick his tongue out, and with both arrogance and brotherly love, tell me to eat dirt.

I pushed my vodka aside and crossed my arms. 'I don't know, I'm confused. He tried to kiss me the other night.'

Jimmy threw both hands up in front of his chest and wiggled his fingers. 'Wooo, not kissing! That's the devil in him, Ruby. Good thing you know when to walk away.'

I squinted. 'I know it seems silly, but this is Lucas we're talking about, not just anybody. I don't want to dig up the past and get all heavy when I'm just going to leave again. It was hard enough the first time. It's easy to slip back into old feelings. The heart remembers what it's like to be in love.'

'And, it would seem'—Jimmy stood and picked up the tray—'what it's like to be broken.'

He turned his back, his voice trailing as he passed a group of pool players who shouted playfully while spilling their beers onto their work boots, and a couple of girls dancing by the juke box as their boyfriends watched adoringly.

I swung my leather jacket over my arm, headed to the door and out into the darkness. I kept my head down and hurried on the footpath with the front door key pressed firmly between my thumb and index finger, as I did every time I walked alone at night.

'If someone was too attack you,' Sam had said when we were about fifteen, 'you could stab them in the eye with your key. Give it a good twist, spit on their squirming face then kick them in the nuts.'

The thought of puncturing an eyeball with a key made me nauseous. I wondered if it would feel like stabbing scissors through a cardboard box or like poking a straw through jelly. Either way, I hoped to never find out.

I was nearly at my parents' home when I spotted a dark figure standing alone in the distance. I lifted the key to my chest and slowed. As I got closer, I recognised Jack, standing at the entrance of his driveway. The shadow of a lemon tree struggling to wave its heavy branches slowly swayed behind him.

'You owe me fifty dollars,' he said as I approached.
'For what?'
'For that dud horse I backed today.'

'I thought you didn't gamble.' I stepped close enough that his breath fell onto my cheek.

'I took a chance,' he said. 'I'll let you off the hook since I owe my first win to you.'

My face felt flushed and my chest heavy. 'I'll make it up to you.'

He inched forward until the hairs on his arm swept against mine.

'Why are you standing outside by yourself. Were you waiting for me?'

Jack didn't answer.

I shrugged and bit my lip, stepping in closer.

He placed his hands on my hips and pulled me in close, his thick body rubbed against my shirt. I lifted my chin to him, noticing how much he towered over me. I felt miniscule wrapped in his arms. I lifted to my tippy toes until my lips met his and lingered for what seemed like seconds. He ran his hand through my hair, rested his finger on my chin and kissed me.

I would have pulled away from any other man with a scotch-tainted tongue, but with Jack, I didn't care. I wanted to know why he drank every night. I wanted to know why he worked out every day. I wanted to know everything. And I wanted more than a kiss. His swept his hands up onto my bare skin at the small of my back, sending an instant shiver up my spine, while his soft lips trailed down the side of my neck until they rested on my collarbone. He lifted his hypnotising blue eyes and, without a word, grabbed my hand and pulled me to his front door.

I looked to my parents' house, the porch light was left on to make it easier for both Jimmy and I to get the key in the front door.

'Are you coming in?' Jack held my hand, his door open.

I squeezed his hand gently, nodded and followed him inside. He pushed open a bedroom door near the entry, and in the dark, grabbed me by the hips and lifted me onto the end of the bed.

Hidden by the darkness, we undressed, pushed the doona aside, and on the sheets, wrapped ourselves around each other. For the first time in a long time, I felt sexy in my own flesh.

His lips lingered on my body, and I traced my fingers over his until I felt a protruding scar above his navel. I froze. It would have been a deep cut. From surgery perhaps, or something more sinister. For a moment, I questioned whether Sam had been right. Maybe he was sketchy. Maybe I should have kept my distance.

But when Jack moved my hands back around his neck, leaned in and whispered, 'Are you okay?', all my sudden worries disappeared. I was okay. I'd let go of all the stresses of life – work, my parents, Lucas. I was, in that moment, completely Jack's.

We lay next to each other, catching our breaths, wrapped in a tangled mess of sheets and pillows, staring blankly at the dark ceiling. When our breathing slowed, Jack turned to me and rested his hand on the slow rise and fall of my stomach.

'That was...'

'Unexpected?'

He laughed and sat up.

'Water?' he asked, leaving the room in the nude.

'Yes, please.' I pulled the sheets up over my chest and grabbed the doona from the floor, straightening it over top.

Jack returned with a glass of water and sat next to me. Was I was expected to stay or leave? If we were in New York, I'd explain how my complicated career left little room for any romantic involvement, then I'd carefully suss out the streets from the windows, sometimes opting to take a back exit, or I'd call a friend to pick me up.

Lucas was the only person I'd felt comfortable staying with overnight. He was my first, and we planned it for weeks in advance. His dad had gone away for the weekend, so I'd packed an overnight bag and told my parents I was staying at Sam's. We lit candles, played music, and clumsily assumed positions. The atmosphere was romantic, but the act was anything but. It got better as our relationship progressed, and soon we were ducking into empty room at parties, restrooms in restaurants and behind bushes on impromptu evening hikes. It was always easy and exciting with Lucas. He had set a precedent for all future lovers.

'I won't stay,' I decided, handing him my empty glass.

He put the glass down and squinted.

'I mean, unless you want me to stay.'

He smiled.

'Do you want me to stay?' I asked hesitantly.

He lay down, leaned on one arm and looked up at me.

I nodded, embarrassed. 'Okay, I'll go.'

Jack raised his hand to my shoulder and slowly pressed until I lay next to him. He leaned in and kissed me gently. The taste of scotch had left his mouth.

I grabbed his hand and turned away, pulling his chest against my back and feeling his nose against my nape.

Twelve

March

It was 6.43 am on the bedside clock when the aromatic smell of coffee shot up my nose, hitting me like a splash of cold water. A glisten of sunlight peeked through the bedroom window.

I wrapped my naked body in the cotton white sheets and adjusted the pillow behind my head to keep the headboard from wobbling. Through half-opened eyes, I surveyed the room as the clanging of dishes sounded from down the hall.

The wooden-panelled room was tiny, crowded. A dark curtain was pulled aside from the double-pane window and a mass of cobwebs hung across the corners of the ceiling. A few clothes, including mine, were strewn across the floor and our empty water glasses sat on the timber bedside table, next to the alarm clock and a faded photo of Jack and two other people.

I picked up the photo and ran my fingers across the dusty glass. He looked young – in his late teens probably. His arms, not covered in ink, were wrapped loosely around the waist of a beautiful girl. She had wide dark eyes, which beamed under the brim of a black hat. Her white teeth shined between bright red lips. The wrinkles beside her eyes showed she was laughing – she must have been. She was too young to have such lines on her face. A guy stood behind them with his hands in the air. He was wearing a backwards hat and had a beer bottle in his hand. White lines ran across the picture from where it had been crinkled then flattened out again. It was barely preserved by the dusty glass in the unpolished silver frame.

'How did you sleep?' Jack stood at the door with two coffee mugs in hand, dressed in only green and blue flannel pyjama pants which hung low on his muscular hips. I looked at his bare chest. It was just as perfect in the sunlight as it was in the dark, but the scar was more prevalent. It was deep red and about three inches long. I put the photo back on the table and tucked my messy hair behind my ears.

'Best sleep I've had in ages.' I shuffled over, careful not to let the sheet slip off my chest. The bed bounced on its flimsy springs as he sat and passed me the mug. I cupped it and breathed in the smell, zapping open my squinty eyes.

'I'm not sure how you take it?'

'This is fine, thanks.' I winced at the black strength. But the mere fact he'd made coffee after a romp was more than any other one-night stand would have done for me. 'How did you sleep?'

'Great, despite the fact I'm not used to having to share a bed.' He smirked.

'Me neither.' I held the hot coffee at bay and re-clenched the sheet under my armpits.

We stared at each other for a moment until he raised his eyebrows and shoulders. 'So, I have to work this morning.'

Like a deer in the headlights, I extended my neck and dropped my mouth open. 'Of course. Of course. I'll get going.'

'There's enough time for you to finish your coffee first.'

I handed it back. 'Thanks, but I really should let you go.' I slipped off the bed and tried to keep the sheets over my body and put on my clothes simultaneously.

'Okay,' he said as I awkwardly clambered in front of him.

I slipped my shoes on and sighed as I realised how ridiculous I'd look walking home with a knotted mane and heels at seven in the morning.

'Nothing says the walk of shame like heels and smudged lipstick.' He laughed.

I looked at his smiling face and traced my index finger over my lips.

'I'm kidding. You don't have smudged lips.'

I pulled my shirt over my head to put it back on.

'You look beautiful.'

I froze with my head buried in my shirt, then pulled it down and looked at him. His eyes were fixated on me and his lips were closed.

He followed me to the front door and opened it. The streets were quiet, the air crisp. The sun was shining but we couldn't feel the heat just yet.

'Okay, well, I guess I will see you around,' I muttered nervously.

'This was fun, right?'

I knew that line. Actually, I had used it often – a classic way to wrap up a session and ensure the other party knew it was nothing serious. For some reason I'd expected it from Jack. It was his disinterest and his mystery that attracted me in the first place. Okay, and maybe his perfect body and stunning blue eyes. I had become infatuated with him. It was a game of cat and mouse. He was a challenge. I had conquered him. I should have hung up the boots. But hearing those words stung. I wanted more. I wanted to feel his hands and lips on me again, I wanted him to stare at me in approval. I wanted to feel wanted, or needed again. And I only wanted it from him.

'Ruby?'

'Yeah, it was fun.'

I walked away through the long grass, manoeuvring over the fallen lemons and prickly weeds. When I reach my front door and turned, Jack was leaning against his open doorway, watching me. I raised a hand.

A PLAN UNRAVELLED

Our outside light was turned off, presumably by Jimmy when he'd finished his evening shift. I cautiously opened the door, hoping no-one was in the kitchen, but both Mum and Dad were sitting at the table, drinking coffee and eating toast. Mum was tapping her toes. Her head jerked around at the sound of the creaky door and she leapt out of her chair.

'Where have you been?' she snapped, like she used to when I was a teen. I hadn't heard her raise her voice in years. Granted, I hadn't been living under their roof for the past fifteen.

'I'm thirty-two,' I said slowly. 'I'm not a teenager.'

'You had me worried.'

'Listen to her. She's a grown adult,' Dad calmly said over his newspaper. 'If she hasn't already learned a thing or two from her lousy life choices, there's no use in us meddling.'

'Somebody needs to meddle,' Mum hit back. 'Maybe if you showed her that you cared about her a little more, she would respect herself a little more and wouldn't make these choices.'

'Respect myself?' My words fell on deaf ears.

'Oh please, that's the stupidest thing I've heard come out of your mouth.' Dad put the paper on the table and tilted his head. 'Actually, no, it's not. You've said a lot of stupid things in your lifetime.'

Mum shook her head. 'Anyway, this isn't about me. It's about Ruby. I was worried about her being out at all hours while in the mental state she's in. That's what mothers do. They worry. They love. They worry some more.'

'Her mental state?' Dad raised his voice.

'My mental state?' Again, my words fell on deaf ears.

'She's not a nutter.' He circled his finger near his temple. I would have appreciated this more if he wasn't so concerned with winning an argument with Mum, rather than lending me his support. 'You are buying into the malicious headlines in those despicable tabloids, which I would read while on the toilet, then wipe my ass with.'

'Do you use sophisticated statements like that in the courtroom?' Mum closed her mouth and tilted her chin in the air.

'It depends on who I'm speaking too. If I'm speaking to uneducated delinquents who don't comprehend full English sentences, then yes, I do.' Dad took a giant bite of toast and chewed while Mum and I stared at him in shock. He swallowed and turned back to Mum. 'You're so innocent, aren't you?'

Mum shot him a look. 'Okay, that's enough now.'

Dad usually had little to say in defence of his own family. He clearly wasn't as pedantic about our public image as Mum was, having not so secretly snuck around with other women, but he had once told us that since he defended so many people at work, he couldn't be bothered doing the same with his own children – he expected better of us.

A PLAN UNRAVELLED

Mum crossed her arms, rubbed her elbows then sat next to Dad, pointing her knees away from him. There was an uncomfortable silence signifying a break in, not an end to, the argument.

'I want what's best for our daughter,' she said softly.

'I'm not so sure,' he muttered.

'What is that supposed to mean?'

Dad's courtroom voice reappeared and his right hand chopped through the air for emphasis. 'It means you are worried about the wrong people getting a hold of the wrong information, and having your daughters face, and our name, dragged through the mud some more.'

'That's not true.' Her defence was severely lacking.

'Bullshit.' Dad put his paper down and the two barked back and forth about how they should treat me and how their public image would be affected. I stood in silence watching them fight like dogs over a bone I had thrown.

Jimmy peeked out his door, and I helplessly stared back. He puffed out his cheeks and rolled his eyes, as though it wasn't the first time he'd heard their howling. I walked up the stairs and, along the way, whispered an apology to Jimmy for the chaos I had created.

'Don't be sorry,' he said quietly. 'New argument, different day. I'm surprised it's taken this long for them to get into it since you've been home. They've been restrained for a month. It's a new record.'

I nodded slightly then dragged my feet to the shower, eavesdropping along the way.

'I am her mother. She's in our care. I have every right to know where she was or who she was with.' Every word was emphasised. 'You know as well as I do that she doesn't want to be here with us, or in Rockford.'

'If Ruby's not happy here, it's because she has an overbearing mother who wants to get her out of the house, then keep her inside, then take her away on a weekend of bonding. You need to back off. She's a grown woman. We can't keep saving her from her poor choices. If she's not happy, she can leave.'

'And go where? She needs compassion, support and forgiveness. We shouldn't punish her with a lifetime of neglect and disrespect.'

'Come on now, are we talking about Ruby, or you?' There was a silence. 'I've been pretty generous by offering an open door. What more do you want?'

More silence.

'I just don't want to see her in trouble.'

The argument stopped, Dad left, and I got in the shower to reluctantly wash away the scent of Jack.

Thirteen

I was twelve, with dad at the Dixon Races, when he'd held up a twenty dollar note and flapped it between his index finger and thumb. It was mine, he'd told me, and I had to choose to either put it all on one horse, or divide it up and place a bet on each race.

I'd studied the form guide and after some thought, told Dad I wanted to place it all on the favourite in the first race. It was a certainty, or so the bookies had me believe, so I planned to pocket the winnings and keep playing with the twenty.

I can't remember the horse's name, but I still recall a clear image of its shiny brown coat, strong hind legs and black flowing mane. The jockey, dressed in purple and white silks, looked focused and determined.

On the top level of the grandstand, I stood on the seat beside Dad, staring through my binoculars and struggling to see over a woman's large red-feathered hat. She batted her eyelashes and puckered her lips as she spoke with the younger man beside her. He smiled politely as she flirted, but the group of friends he was with had less tact, making cougar comments and catcalls. The woman was oblivious to anyone around her, including Dad, who had to sway several times to avoid being attacked by her flashy headdress.

But all the attention turned to the track when the horses left the barrier in a thunderous start. My heart raced and I shouted out as my pick overtook the rest, but as it came around the bend, approaching the finish line, the jockey lost control. There was a synchronised gasp from the crowd. I let the binoculars go and they hung from my neck, my stomach rose to my throat and my hands fell to my side as I watched the horse crash into the barrier and throw the jockey onto the track below.

We watched quietly as a crew of people rushed to both the jockey and the horse. After several minutes, the jockey miraculously walked away uninjured, waving to an applauding crowd. But the horse lay still. I swallowed the lump in my throat as a tarp was raised.

'That's it? They're going to kill it?' I asked.

'How do I explain this to you in a way you would understand?' Dad bent over until his face was inches from mine. 'It's like in show business. What does every show have in common?'

I scratched my head.

'Think, Ruby. It has a beginning, an entertaining middle then an end. Some shows are longer, some are shorter. Some are funny and beautiful and make you laugh and some are sad and tragic. Eventually, whether we are ready or not, the lights go out and the curtains will close. Or in this case, the tarp is raised.' He stood and patted the race book in his open palm. He snickered. 'Off to the glue factory.'

Besides learning how callous Dad could be, I also learned some valuable lessons that day: nothing in life is a certainty, but death; the things you expect to bring you the biggest joy could turn into the biggest tragedies; the favourite doesn't always win; and sometimes it pays to take a risk and back a horse which has the odds stacked against it.

Little did I know those lessons would come into play twenty years later, as I sat in my bedroom looking at a picture of Lucas, then out the window at Jack's house. The safe bet and the dark horse.

Since I'd left Jack's house, I'd hung on every moment, hoping to hear from him.

Yet I was unwilling to tell Sam about our tryst, because I knew she wouldn't approve; her money was on Lucas. She'd called to talk about Lucas, and about Harry, and we'd made more double date plans.

I wanted to tell Jimmy. Growing up, I'd confided in him about men. But this time I didn't. And I definitely didn't let Michelle catch wind of my escapades, when she'd called to see how I was going and to keep me up to date with all her work since I'd left New York.

'I checked in on your apartment. I sent a cleaner around to keep the dust out and the floors polished.' I could hear the bustle of a crowd around her. We'd had numerous, similar conversations where she juggled an espresso in one hand and designer bag around her bent, pointed elbows, which nudged anyone taking up too much space on the footpaths. 'I also spoke with the editor of Entertainment Digest and The Star Report. They agreed to cull any prospective stories or photos in exchange for a tell-all. And they're paying big bucks, Anna, so that should help with the dwindling bank account. Speaking of, I've run the numbers and we have enough to get you through to September. That covers mortgage payments, bills, food, necessities. And me. Then with interviews, photo shoots and whatnot you should be fine. Just no big purchases, okay?'

Again, I was being spoken to like a child. I didn't answer.

'Okay?'

'Yup, got it.'

'Good, now back to what I was saying before, we will rehearse everything you need to say during these interviews, so don't stress. It'll just be about how it was completely accidental, you left to find time for yourself and to visit family, blah blah blah. I've got a hold of some paparazzi photos. Paid a bit of a price, but it's my gift to you. I don't know how they got their mitts on pictures of you in hospital. Some asshole who works there obviously leaked them, but I've got an investigator looking into it. And then I set up a meeting...'

Michelle was impassive, organised and to the point. Like the stereotypical New York taxi driver, she would find the most direct route from A to B, do her best to avoid any detours or distractions and would blast her horn if anyone tried to slow her down.

So I did think twice before I interrupted her, because even though I was her boss, Michelle had no problem pressing on the gas and knocking me down when I made alternative suggestions. This time though, I struggled with her planned route.

'I'm not so sure a tell-all is a good idea,' I said, sparking her brakes and forcing a rare silence. 'And, I don't think we need to investigate the pictures. Maybe we should just let it all blow over.'

'Um, Anna. People don't just forget these things. This won't just blow over. I thought we had an agreement. You go to Australia; I work out this mess you made. And this is me working out the mess you made. We can't just ignore this. We have to face it head on, then move on.'

The thought of appearing in front of a camera and discussing the incident was humiliating. 'Maybe I'm just not ready yet.'

'Of course you aren't ready.' I could hear her heels clunking across the pavement again. 'This is why you needed to get away. Clear your head. Take a break. Then, when you come back, I'll have your apartment ready, your fridge stocked, and your routine back in order. We'll rehearse any interviews I've scheduled and get back into scripts and castings and all that fun stuff you're probably missing right now, right?'

'I guess.' I looked to my tapping toes. Damn my mother's habits.

'You guess? Okay, well, you don't sound convinced. But you don't pay me the big bucks for nothing. Although right now, you can barely afford me.' She laughed. 'Okay, I gotta go. There's a new drop at Givenchy, and I heard it's selling fast.'

'Maybe I need to reassess your salary,' I muttered.

'Oh, darling,' Michelle said, putting on a posh voice, 'I'm giving you a bargain. Anyway, enjoy your time away and put your feet up for a while. Well, not literally. We can't have you coming back looking like an Oompa-Loompa now, can we? I'll call you in a couple weeks with another update. You take care of yourself, mmkay?'

I hung up, buried my face in my hands and groaned. I wanted to act again, but my passion, and the longing for success I once had, was now replaced with shame and a fear of ridicule. My brain ached thinking about whether the industry would accept me again, or whether I was ready to go back to the bustling lifestyle.

I needed some air.

I tied the laces of my bright runners then ran hard, my emotions flowing out of my body through a stream of sweat and tears until my knees got weak and my ankles ached.

A PLAN UNRAVELLED

'You were gone for a while.' Ron was kneeling in his garden bed, near the footpath, as I returned.

'I didn't see you when I left,' I said between deep breaths. I wiped the sweat from under my white baseball cap and walked to him.

He took off his blackened gardening gloves, stretched his green-stained knees and brushed his forearm against his forehead. 'It's good to see you taking care of yourself.'

'I always take care of myself, or try to I guess,' I panted. 'Contrary to popular belief.'

'I didn't mean to offend.'

I took a deep breath, bent over and grabbed my knees. 'Running's a good stress reliever.'

'Maybe I should start running then. I could do with some stress relief.'

'You just got back from travelling the world. What could you possibly be stressed about?' I stretched my arms in the air clasped my hands above my head, enjoying a stretch down my spine.

He sighed. 'Life, Ruby. Life.'

'I hear ya.' I stuck out my leg and stretched my calf muscle.

'I better dust my runners off and pound the pavement. One foot in front of the other.' He put his gloves back on. 'So tell me, what's got you down?'

'Nothing and everything.' I switched legs.

He stared, waiting for more.

'I don't know. Trying to decide between the familiar and the unknown. Mum always said there was comfort in the familiar.'

'Ah, yes. She told me that once too.' He looked to Mum and Dad's front door, then back at me. 'I was about your age when I had a big choice to make between the two.'

'What did you choose?'

'It doesn't matter.' He looked at his feet. 'What I chose didn't choose me.'

'I'm sorry.'

'Don't be,' he said. 'I've got my health, I travelled the world, I'm lucky.'

I smiled.

'You know what? Maybe I don't need to go running.'

I walked to the house, shouting over my shoulder. 'Do it anyway. It's good for you.'

FOURTEEN

I puckered my lips then checked my teeth as Mum answered a knock at the front door. That would be Lucas. With high hopes but low expectations, I rummaged through my bag and checked my mobile to see if Jack had called. Hopes dashed.

'Oh, Lucas, wonderful to see you again.'

'Same to you, Mrs Johns. You haven't aged a bit.'

'Oh, Lucas.' Mum simpered. 'Now tell me. What have you been doing with yourself these days?'

I stood on the top step, peered over the railing and watched quietly. Lucas's hair fell softly on his cheek. His black jacket made his big brown eyes stand out and his thick curly hair shine. I had told him years ago that dark clothes looked good on him. I wondered if his attire was a coincidence, or if he remembered.

'Well,' he rubbed his hands together, 'work and work I guess. I've been enjoying my move back. I missed it here.'

'I haven't seen you around, then again, Rockford's grown a bit. But I bet it's nice to be back,' Mum said endearingly. 'The slow pace, the friendly faces.'

'Yes,' Lucas said as he caught me standing at the top of the stairs, so I had no choice but to walk down to join them. 'You can't go past the Rockford people,' he continued.

Mum looked up and smiled. The last time she watched me walk down the stairs towards Lucas was for my high school formal. I had worn a bright-red dress, my hair was pulled back into tight curls and I'd gripped the railing tight as I tried to balance on red stilettos, which I hadn't yet mastered. Lucas wore a black suit, white shirt and red tie to match my dress. He slipped a corsage on my wrist and kissed me on the cheek, careful not to show too much affection in front of my dad, who took pictures of us for the event. It was the first night Lucas had told me he loved me and it was the first time I said it back.

'Well, you two have a good night. I won't wait up this time,' Mum said. 'If I had known you were staying with Lucas the other night I wouldn't have been so worried.'

Lucas turned to me, his mouth half open, but I anxiously looked past him, opened the door and led the way to his car. As I buckled my seatbelt, I waited for him to question me. Should I explain, or make an excuse?

But he didn't. He strapped on his seatbelt and reversed out the driveway. 'You look really good.'

I sighed and avoided peering out my passenger window to Jack's house.

A PLAN UNRAVELLED

We ate lunch at a small café I hadn't been to before, though it had been in Rockford for years. The waitress knew most of the patrons by name, and by the way she smiled at me, I assumed she knew who I was too.

Lucas told me stories about the cases he worked on, and I told him what he wanted to know about the actors and actresses I brushed shoulders with. While most of my colleagues were classified as emerging or B-grade, I had attended some events with A-listers and had a few stories up my sleeve.

He insisted on paying again, and because we had only been at the café for over an hour, he suggested ice cream after.

'Ice cream?' I sounded like a ten-year-old. 'I haven't had ice cream for so long.'

'Well, I could try to get you drunk, but it's a Sunday afternoon so that might not be appropriate. Ice cream seems a bit more responsible,' he said. 'And it's hot out.'

'Well it is hot out.' I walked by his side, clasping onto my bag. 'That's one good argument. Secondly, I can't say no to ice cream.'

We walked a couple streets until we got to the ice cream shop. I was taken back by the owner, a middle-aged woman with a protruding collarbone, grey hair pulled underneath a net, and a few large boils over her chin and nose. But I couldn't help but smile when she grinned excitedly and handed me a large waffle cone with lopsided strawberry ice cream dripping down the side. 'They're on me,' she beamed.

Her enthusiasm was infectious. 'Well, thank you.'

'No, thank you. What a pleasure to have you in our shop!'

I nodded in appreciation.

'So I just need to take you with me whenever I need a freebie,' Lucas joked as he licked chocolate off the side of his cone. We went outside and sat on chairs at a small table for two.

'Maybe she gave us these freebies because she's keen on you.' I laughed.

'Ha. She's just my type. Should I go back there and get her number?' He elbowed me.

I felt a sense of guilt for making fun of her appearance. 'We're not nice,' I said. 'Too bad we all couldn't just look past the exterior. She seemed quite lovely.'

'You're right,' Lucas agreed. 'And she is obviously a fan of yours.'

The child at the market, the whispers at the restaurant, the waitress at the café and the ice cream lady. Perhaps more people recognised me than I'd thought. The difference was, they were subtler in Rockford than they were in New York. 'I don't know how I feel about being recognised here.'

'Is that why you cut your hair off?'

'This?' I ran my free hand over the top of my short hair. 'Maybe. Maybe I just needed a change.'

He laughed.

'What?' I asked.

'You, change? We had to practically push you out of the country to chase your dreams. Then, I am guessing, if you're the same girl I knew in high school, you probably followed a strict routine. The same wake up time. The same study time. The same gym time. Ate a strict diet.'

'Hey...'

'Sorry, but not sorry. Am I right?' His ice cream was dripping to the pavement beside his toes.

'I guess.'

'You guess?' he asked playfully.

'Damn it, Lucas,' I tapped the table with the tip of my cone. 'You know me too well. Even after all these years.'

He pointed to his head. 'It's all locked away up here. I remember.'

I took a bite of my ice cream and shuffled in my chair.

'So, am I right about the hair then?'

I swallowed and turned to him. 'Yeah. You're right,' I caved. 'I don't think I am getting recognised for the right reasons anymore.'

'Everyone knows you, Ruby. And they know you for your talent. They're not concerned about the bad stuff.'

'I can only hope.'

'You made me real proud. I always knew you would make it.'

I looked at him. 'You did?'

'Yeah, of course. You were destined for big things.' He popped the last bit of cone in his mouth and wiped his fingers on the serviette. He waited until he was finished and composed to continue. 'As much as I wanted you to stay, I didn't want to hold you back.'

'Why didn't you tell me you wanted me to stay?' I asked between my final bites.

'Haven't you heard the saying... if you love somebody, let them go?'

'I've heard it.'

He rested his arm on the table. 'And if you had stayed, you would have always wondered what could have been. You needed to go find yourself and achieve your dreams.'

As we drove home, I looked out at the empty streets and large, lush lawns. 'I like the grass.'

Lucas raised an eyebrow. 'What?'

I realised how silly I sounded and laughed too. 'Nobody has a front lawn in New York.'

Lucas ceased his laughing as he turned into the driveway and put the car in park. He rubbed his hands together then looked at me with wide eyes and a soft grin. 'I'd try to kiss you again, but seeing as how you stayed somewhere else the other night, I'm tipping we're on different pages.'

A PLAN UNRAVELLED

I wrongfully thought I was in the clear. 'What?' I asked, uncomfortably.

'Hey. I probably should have addressed the elephant in the room when your mum brought it in.' He grinned. 'I don't mean to pry or anything, and you don't have to explain anything to me.'

I bit my lip, unsure of what to say next.

'I know you've been through a lot lately, and moving back to Rockford is a huge change.' His voice cracked. 'It would take a while to adjust, to sort your life out, get settled... I don't know what I am trying to say.'

I put my hand on his to steady his nerves.

'I want you to know that even after all these years, I am here for you, as your friend. And if you decide that maybe you want to take things further, then...'

'I had a really good time.' I leaned over and gave him a lingering kiss on the cheek to stop any further rambling. 'Thank you.'

He mouthed, 'Bye, Ruby,' then waited in his car until I closed the door behind me.

FIFTEEN

I kept my phone within arm's reach. Even while in the shower. I sat it near the basin, or on my folded towel. I even carried it to the toilet, despite the fact my whereabouts would be quite obvious if Jack ended up calling me while I was midstream.

I placed the phone beside my open laptop as I sat at my desk, scrolling through entertainment websites on my computer, hoping I wouldn't come across photos or articles about the fall of Anna Johns. There was a time in my life when I excitedly welcomed news from Michelle that my name or photo was in print, but now I cringed at what captions would follow.

I had my door propped open slightly. Mum's soap opera was on the television downstairs and Jimmy was strumming his guitar in his bedroom. I was enjoying his acoustic medley when a firm knock repeated on the front door.

'Hello? Can I help you?' Mum asked hesitantly.

'Uh, is Ruby here?'

I threw my hand over my mouth and swung my chair around. Jack!

'Yes, she is. Is she expecting you?'

I pulled at my shirt, breathed into my hand and sniffed to ensure my breath was fresh, then quickly checked my hair in the mirror and made sure there were no remnants of my bacon, tomato and spinach sandwich wedged between my teeth.

'I don't think so,' he said.

'Hey.' I smiled, all calm and collected as I walked downstairs.

'Uh, hey.' He shifted awkwardly under the doorway, with his arms behind his back.

Mum glanced between us.

'Um, sorry to just drop in. I thought you might need this.' He pulled out my vintage ruby and diamond ring.

A knot formed in my stomach. How could I leave something so valuable behind and not take any notice? I took the ring from him and put it on my index finger. 'I didn't even realise it was missing.'

'Oh, oh.' Mum's eyes were wide as if she had just solved a puzzle. 'You're a friend?'

'Jack,' he said.

I made a face at Mum and she pursed her lips and took a step back.

'Okay.' He tucked his hands in his pockets and turned away.

'Do you want to come in for a coffee?' I asked.

He looked back at me, then Mum. 'Uh, that's okay, I should get going.'

Mum stepped forward and, sensing my desperation, pleaded. 'Please come in, Jack. I've just boiled the kettle and I made a sponge cake yesterday that has barely been touched.'

His dimples appeared. 'Well, I can't refuse cake.'

Mum retrieved three mugs from the kitchen cupboard. 'I've seen you come and go next door, Jack, but you are never outside long enough for me to say hello,' she called over her shoulder. 'How do you take your coffee?'

'Just black, thank you.'

'And would you like tea or coffee, Ruby?'

'Coffee, please.' I guided Jack to the table.

'Okay, one black and one white,' she said, adding milk to mine. Jack's eyes met mine and he smiled.

'White?' he mouthed.

I walked to the pantry, grabbed the sponge cake, cut three slices and popped each one on a plate.

'So, Jack, what do you do?' Mum handed him his mug.

'I work at the mines.'

'I should have guessed. Seems everyone I don't know around here comes from somewhere else to work at the mines. Plus, I've seen you in your work gear.'

'Mmmm.' He sipped his coffee then set it on the table, twisting it back and forth like he did with his scotch.

I passed him the cake and a fork, then went back to the kitchen to get the other two plates.

'You must be a relative of Mrs Williams?'

'She was my grandmother.'

'Oh, well I am sorry.'

'For what?'

'Because she's dead.'

There was an awkward silence as I sat next to Mum and poked my cake.

'Uh, we weren't close. In fact, I didn't know she existed until the lawyer contacted me to notify me of her death and give details of her will.'

'Oh, well, that's a shame,' Mum said nervously. 'I would have never guessed she had children. There were never any visitors while she lived there.'

'She had a son. They weren't close.'

'Your father?'

He didn't answer.

'Are you close with your father and mother?' Her small talk had rapidly transformed into a deep and meaningful.

'Mum,' I muttered, hoping she would quit.

'Not really.'

'Oh.' Mum ignored my plea. 'Do you have brothers or sisters?'

'Nope.'

Mum's toe started tapping. 'Oh, well, it's just you then?'

'Basically.'

Mum searched for something more to say.

'Have you lived here all your life?' he asked before she could pry further.

'All our lives,' she said. 'Except Ruby, of course. She still doesn't technically live here, she says. She won't call this place home.' She broke into nervous laughter.

He shook his head and squinted his eyes.

'I'm going back to New York in a couple months.'

He lifted his chin. 'Interesting.'

I forced a grin, then took several swigs of hot coffee. He took a large bite of his cake and we sat quietly.

'So, do you enjoy the mines?' Mum asked, unable to cope with the silence.

'It's alright,' he said with a mouthful. 'It gets me by.'

'Yes, well, it must be good money for you to come to Rockford from… wherever it is you came from…' She waved her hand in a circular motion.

'Brisbane.'

'Brisbane,' she smiled. 'Beautiful.'

We all stared at each other and into our empty plates, unable to hide behind our forks.

'Well. I guess I best be doing something. I've got laundry to fold and toilets to clean. I like to keep a clean house.' Mum stood and collected our plates, then gave Jack a fleeting glance. 'And a tidy yard.'

My face felt hot.

'It was nice to meet you,' he said. Once she was out of sight, he caught my gaze and grinned.

'That's my mum.' I raised my eyebrows. 'You survived her grilling. Congratulations.'

'She seems nice.'

'She means well.'

'So, you're just living here temporarily?' His voice was a little louder and unbroken, and his shoulders dropped.

'Yes. Yes, definitely temporarily. I can't live in my parents' house forever.'

'I mean, in Australia. You go back to New York soon?'

'Yeah.' I sighed. 'Yeah, that's my home, I guess. I've been there for half my life. This is just a little bit of a break.'

'Do you miss it?'

I stopped to ponder. Do I? The bright lights, the culture, the stage. Yes. But I don't miss the long and strenuous hours, the relentless paparazzi and the vicious tabloids. 'A bit. Do you miss Queensland?'

'No.'

'Do your friends come to visit?'

He went quiet and the brightness in his eyes faded. 'I like to keep to myself for the most part.'

I opened my mouth to ask more, but he was too quick. 'So, what were you doing in America?'

I sighed. I didn't want to divulge too much information to the one person in my life who seemed to know nothing about my scandal. But he was trying to make conversation, and with no family in Rockford, and presumably no friends, I suspected he didn't have many genuine chats.

'I was an actress,' I caved. 'I am an actress.'

'Ads? Television? Movies?' He paused. 'Porn?'

I rolled my eyes. 'I started in Broadway then moved to film. Not exotic.' I laughed. 'Just regular, run-of-the-mill movies. No nudity. Dad made it a clause in my contract years ago, and it just stuck.'

'So you don't get naked easily, then?' He smirked. 'I feel privileged.'

I smirked too, turning the ring back and forth.

'That explains how you can afford that.' He pointed to my finger.

'In actual fact, I probably couldn't afford it. I got a little over excited when I received my first pay check.' I was telling him too much. My finances weren't his business.

He stared at his fingers and smiled. I coughed and his eyes snapped back to meet mine.

'So, Ruby Johns. Romance? Comedies? Horrors?'

'Drama, comedy, action, a bit of everything I supposed. Nothing earth shattering. A couple that broke the box office, a lot that went straight to DVD,' I said. 'And I'm Anna Johns in the industry.'

'Anna?' he spat. 'Why Anna?'

'Well, when I first went to America and found my agent, slash publicist, slash everything, really... Michelle... she suggested we change my name to something that rolled off the tongue... Joanna Johns.'

Jack's lips parted.

'Then, after some deliberation, she thought Joanna sounded too old. I was only just out of high school. So she shorted in to Anna Johns.'

'So, just plucked a name out of thin air? It wasn't your middle name or your great Aunt's name? Nothing?'

'Nothing. Then I got cast in a Broadway show and we started getting calls for Anna Johns and scripts for Anna Johns. By the time I was twenty-one, I'd forgotten who Ruby was. Then I got my first movie deal and I bought the ring. It was meant to be a reminder of who I was before I got to New York: Ruby.'

He sat quietly studying everything I had revealed. 'So, Broadway? You sing and dance and stuff?'

'Yeah,' I said. 'Well, I used to sing and dance, and stuff. Then when I stopped doing live theatre, I stopped practicing. I barely sing anymore, unless I'm in the shower.'

'Well, I'd like to hear you sometime,' he said. 'In the shower.'

I giggled. 'Maybe, one day.'

Mum walked by carrying a tower of freshly folded towels. 'Don't mind me.'

Once she was up the stairs, Jack stood and stretched his arms. 'Well, I should get going.'

I stood too. 'Okay.'

'Do you have any plans?'

♥

The inside of his house was tidier than I remembered, and I hoped he had cleaned with expectations of me returning. I followed him to the living room. The pale blue walls looked like they hadn't seen a coat of fresh paint since the house was built, nearly fifty years ago. The worn furniture didn't fare much better, the colours clashing.

'Sorry, this place isn't the nicest.' He sank into the centre of the couch, leaving little room for me. I sat on the matching chair next to it and curled my feet up. The movement sent dust into the air, causing me to sneeze. I wiped the grey particles from the sides of my jeans. I would have worn my shorts on such a hot day, but they were a bit snug.

'It's homely,' I said.

'Probably a bit different to your New York apartment.'

'I didn't spend a lot of time there, anyway.'

'A bit of a socialite?'

'Workaholic, more like it.'

He stared blankly. 'Well, you must be enjoying the break then.'

I clenched my teeth and swallowed. Jack turned the television on and flicked through the music channels, stopping at classic rock.

'Don't you watch normal TV?'

'Nah.' He rested the remote on his coffee table, next to a glass with brown residue in the bottom. 'Or movies. Hence why I had no idea who you were.'

'Well, it's a bit refreshing, actually.'

'Yeah?'

'Yeah.' I grinned. 'Most people don't seem to really care about me here anyway.'

He scratched his neck.

'It's been an adjustment. Good, I guess. A bit of a hideaway.'

Jack leaned back and placed his hands on his wide-spread knees. 'That it is.'

'So, we're just going to sit back and listen to music all afternoon? I could have done that from the sole comfort of my childhood bedroom,' I said.

'Well, I can come up with something else to do,' he bit his lip and looked from my toes to my face.

'Me too.' I dropped my feet and inched my bum to the edge of the seat. He came closer. I'm not giving in just yet. 'Cards!'

He threw his head back. 'Cards? Like, a card game?'

'Yes, like a card game. I can't remember the last time I played.'

'Me neither. And there is probably a reason for it.'

'C'mon. Humour me for a while.'

After a slight hesitation, Jack stood and walked to the kitchen.

'Where are you going?'

He didn't say anything, but I heard rummaging through drawers. He returned with a deck of cards and two glasses of water.

'My grandmother's, not mine,' he handed me the pack and set the drinks down.

I took the crisp cards out of the faded package and shuffled them. 'Did she leave you everything?'

'No, my dad.'

'And he gave it to you?'

'In a way.' He sipped his water.

I stopped shuffling, set the cards on the coffee table and waited, ready to hear more... wanting so badly to hear more.

'Let's play war.' He cleared his throat, grabbed the cards and dealt. 'It's the only one I really know. You aren't going to encourage me to bet on this too?'

'Maybe.' I knelt in front of the table and Jack followed. 'What's your wager?'

He rubbed his chin, the short stubble on his sharp cheeks rustling against his hand. I stared at his eyes and, drawn in, caught my breath.

'If I win, you have to re-enact one of your favourite scenes.'

I burst into laughter. 'No way.'

'Why not?'

'I'm on a break from work.'

'What about a song?'

I hesitated. 'Fine, why not? I don't lose anyway.'

He pumped his fist as if he had already won.

'And if I win, you have to...' I struggled to think of a wager. 'Um... do fifty push-ups.'

He laughed. 'Well, okay. You're on.'

We leant across the table, throwing competitive faces at each other while flipping through our cards. My shoulders tensed with every move until we both played aces. I slapped my hand down and shouted. 'War!'

I won with a king and snickered as I gathered the pile.

'Oh, bloody hell. There's still plenty to go. Don't count yourself so lucky just yet. Anything can happen.'

After several rounds, Jack was down to only a small handful of cards, and with each war, I plucked them from him.

'Haven't played in years, my ass.' He leaned against the couch and admitted defeat. 'You were quicker than lightening. I think you told me a fib.'

I folded my cards on the table and pointed to the carpet in front of me. 'On all fours, mister.'

He crawled towards me and I turned sideways to watch him. He slowly stretched his arms and legs out and raised his shoulders off the ground. His veins popped under his tattoos, triceps bulging, and his shirt clung to his shoulders and broad back. 'Fifty?'

'Fifty,' I mouthed, admiring how close he was.

He pushed down so his nose grazed the carpet, pushed back up again, then continued, counting out loud. His cologne was subtle but tantalising. He looked to me with soft eyes and a half-smile.

'You can stop now,' I whispered into his cheek after about a dozen push-ups.

He rolled to his side.

'You probably didn't wake up this morning thinking you would be doing that today,' I said.

'I never wake up with expectations.'

'Why is that?'

'If you don't have any expectations, you can't be disappointed.' Jack scooped his finger around the hairs hanging loose over my face and lifted them behind my ear. His cheeks sunk in as he swallowed. His hand slipped from my ear to behind my neck and he pulled me in closer, kissing me softly. Every calculated move made my body tingle, my stomach drop, my fingertips tickle and my head blurry. But then he pulled back, like he'd suddenly remembered something.

'Sorry.'

'Is everything alright?'

'I don't want you to get the wrong idea. I'm not after anything serious.'

I knew that. I knew from his secrets. I knew when he walked me out of his house the other night. I knew it, and I was meant to be okay with it. But once again, I wasn't. I wanted more. I wanted as much as I could get before I had to go back. But I couldn't let him know.

A PLAN UNRAVELLED

'If we don't have expectations, we can't be disappointed, right?' I pulled him back to me. Within minutes our clothes were strung across the floor, and I was left sweaty and breathless, wrapped up in his arms, oblivious to the rough, old stained carpet under my bare back.

I ran my hand over his chest and down to his scar. He grabbed my fingers and intertwined them in his. Was his turned head meant to avoid my gaze?

It didn't take long for him to fall asleep, unfazed by sunlight through the window, the itchy carpet, or the nineties music still sounding in the background. The clock ticked to 5 pm. I eased Jack's arm up, slid out from under him, then slipped on my clothes and combed my fingers through my knotty hair.

I headed to the toilet and, on my way back, was drawn to the photo in his bedroom. I picked it up and studied his wrinkled nose, his straight teeth and his squinty eyes as he laughed. It was beautiful.

'You like that picture.' Jack stood at the doorway, clothed, a red patch on his cheek from where it had been pressed against the floor. He rubbed his eyes. 'How long was I asleep?'

'Only half an hour.'

'Is that all? Seems like it's been hours.'

'You must have had a deep sleep.'

'You must have tired me out.'

I looked back at the picture, then at him. 'You look so happy in this photo.'

'I was.'

'And young.'

'I was.'

'Good friends?'

He nodded.

'Do they live in Queensland still?'

'They're dead,' he said flatly. 'You hungry?'

Sixteen

'We apparently have our own pool, a buffet breakfast every morning and a butler on call. A BUTLER ON CALL!' Sam passed me the brochure of a Fijian hotel she and Harry had booked for a holiday. She'd stopped by the house this morning with a cheeky grin and a picnic basket. So here we were, sitting on a purple picnic rug in one of Rockford's few parks, enjoying Sam's idea of lunch: crackers, cheese, grapes, a couple plastic cups and a cheap bottle of Moscato. I poured the wine.

I squinted at the glistening leaflet and slid my sunnies from my hair to my eyes. 'Sounds pretty romantic.' I handed it back to her. 'Maybe he'll propose?'

She rolled onto her stomach, kicked her feet up and crossed her ankles in the air. 'I know, right? I've been dropping hints.' She twirled her long hair around her index finger like she used to do in high school. 'I even left the website of a jeweller up on our computer the other day, for him to see.'

'Subtle, Sam.'

She giggled.

'If that's not a dead giveaway, I don't know what is.'

'Exactly. I don't know what else I have to do to get him to pop the question.' She held her hand in the air and spread out her fingers.

'Well, I am glad you're happy.' I curled my thumb against the ruby ring on my index finger.

'I'm happy. Very happy.' She flipped onto her back and pulled her shoulder straps down in an attempt to get an even tan. 'Funny, isn't it?'

'What?'

'I don't know. I guess everyone thought this day would never come.'

'What do you mean?' I knew exactly what she meant, and she knew it.

'The wild child. The high school dropout. The druggie.'

'Everyone goes through a phase, some more than others,' I said. 'You went back to school, you stopped partying and you own a bustling business. You should be proud of yourself.'

She let out a bogus laugh. 'A pub. I own a pub.'

'A busy pub.'

'You know what my parents said when I bought the pub?'

I dug my elbow into the blanket and propped my head on my hand. 'Good for you?'

'Right. They shook their head and asked Father Brown to talk to me.'

'Father Brown? Your old priest?'

'Yeah, our priest. He still is the priest, actually. He struggles and I can barely make out a word he says. Between us, I think he may have a few extra swigs of the wine before the congregation arrives.'

'What? You go to church?'

'Yes, I go to church! Believe it or not!'

'I don't believe it.' Who is this woman?

'Well, I do. I've been going ever since I went back to high school. It made me feel at peace, you know? It was therapeutic, and still is.' She sat up again and threw her arms around her bent knees. 'Anyway. They asked Father Brown to give me a lecture about being loose. Drinking, drugs, sex, rock and roll.' She laughed. 'Him, the closet wine hog.'

'Can you say that about a priest?' I asked.

'I don't know. Maybe God will make me scrub the floors and clean the gates before I'm allowed into Heaven. We'll see. Anyway, back to my story please.'

'Proceed.'

'My parents think I'm just the worst person around. The worst. I told Father Brown that things had changed, and how I'd got my act together, and he believed me. He gave me some advice about keeping my life on track, that sort of thing. Despite all this, my parents stopped talking to me.'

'What?'

'Yup. Haven't spoken to them in years. See them at church, we don't even wave hello. They think I am going there to try and prove a point. That it's all an act. You know I can't act. That was always your territory.' She grinned. 'They think I'm poison and that I'm poisoning everyone who steps foot in the pub. They think I can't be trusted. If they knew we were here, drinking in the park, in the middle of the day... Wowee! And if they knew I was feeding you alcohol – you of all people...'

She looked at me as she had just slapped me across the face, and I dropped my jaw as if she had.

'I'm sorry.'

'I'm allowed to drink.'

'Are you?' she asked.

'I'm not an alcoholic, Sam. I'm not a drug addict.'

She threw me a doubtful look.

'I'm not,' I insisted. 'I was just trying to keep up. Fulfil expectations. I was always after everyone's approval and didn't want to let anyone down.' I looked at my ring. 'Ha. Look how that turned out.'

'I think you fulfilled everyone's expectations and achieved your childhood dreams,' she said. 'Now it's time to focus on what you want.'

I lay back on the blanket and folded my arms behind my head. 'I'm not so sure what that is.'

'I know what you want.'

'What?' This'll be good.

'Some loving! I know it makes me feel better.' she laughed.

It would have been a good time to tell her about Jack, but I didn't. Instead, my face told her for me. A sign my acting had gone downhill since I'd left New York.

'Oh. My. Word. You have gotten laid, haven't you?' she sat up and shook her finger at me. 'Lucas hasn't said a word about it. What a gentleman!'

I rolled my eyes and held up my hand. 'Shhh. And no, not Lucas.'

'What?!' she shrieked, then lowered her voice. 'Who?'

'Promise not to lecture me?'

She raised her hand to her heart. 'Promise.'

'That hot guy in your pub that you said was sketchy.'

She rolled her eyes as she scrambled to figure out who I was talking about, then dropped her mouth and widened her eyes. 'Him? Scotch-drinking miner guy? I told you not him!'

I scrunched my nose. 'Why not? You don't know a thing about him.'

'Well, enlighten me. What do you know about him?'

'Uh, that his name is Jack. That he's Mrs William's grandson. That he works at the mines, is from Brisbane and...'

'Why did he leave Brisbane? Does he have any friends or family around? What does he do for fun?'

'I don't know,' I said defensively. I wish I had the answers. 'It's not like we know everything about each other just yet. We're having fun.'

'Well, I think you need to have a serious conversation with him. I bet he won't tell you shit. Everyone says he's hiding something shady, and I don't get a good vibe from him.'

'I get a good vibe from him,' I joked, hoping to spread a smile. It didn't work.

'Now I have to worry about you.'

'The tables have turned, haven't they?' I picked up the empty plates and glasses and packed them into the picnic basket. 'He's introverted. May come off shady to those who don't know him, but he's actually a nice guy.'

'You know, Lucas has friends who could run a quick background search on him for you. You can ask him tonight, at dinner.'

'No!' I snapped. 'How is Lucas going to feel if I ask him to run a search on a guy I'm sleeping with? And another thing, who said I was coming to dinner?'

'I did. I invited Lucas yesterday, and I'm inviting you now,' she said. 'But if you do want Lucas to do it, he would, for you. Lucas would do anything for you.'

I stared, silently pleading with her to give it up.

'I'll say no more.'

Lucas and Harry were sitting on bar stools at Sam's kitchen bench, pulling at pieces of warm crusty bread and dipping them in a bowl of balsamic vinegar and olive oil, as Sam stood near the oven, tossing a salad. Her small house smelled of garlic and onion and her block-out curtains were drawn, shielding out the sunny evening it was. Perhaps she was trying to create some ambience.

Sam's white round table barely fit inside the kitchen, its surface dressed with four placemats, plates and wine glasses. Sam herself looked surprising – a refined domestic goddess in a red floral apron tied over her black curve-hugging mini dress. Her hair was pulled back into a top knot, highlighting her plump cheeks and full lips. The scars on her face were visible, but not ugly. I wondered if she'd forgotten to layer her make-up, or whether she left her skin exposed on purpose.

The three of them had been discussing Fiji, when I arrived. Lucas smiled at me, but didn't stand to kiss my cheek or give me a hug, as he had on our previous dates. He pulled out the seat next to him, and I sat, crossed my legs and grabbed at the bread.

Lucas said he had been to Fiji several times with his ex-wife. Every time he brought her up, he gave me a fleeting look. I didn't know if he expected the mere mention of her to make me jealous, but in actual fact, I was glad he hadn't been alone all these years. I felt sad for him – that he wasn't still with her, that he didn't have children or the picture-perfect life he had envisioned when we were young.

'Two dogs, three kids, a white picket fence and a Tarago,' he'd said to me once when we were camping with his cousins. He was skipping rocks on the river while I sat next to him on the river bank. 'And, of course, a Lamborghini for me. I'll drive behind to make sure you guys arrive at our holiday house safely.'

Harry raised his glass. 'You know where else I would love to go? Spain.'

'I've been there too,' Lucas said.

Harry nudged him. 'You've been everywhere. Guess I should have been a lawyer instead of a tradie.'

'Nah,' Sam chimed in. 'You look sexy with a hard-on. I mean a hardhat on.'

We all laughed, and I could feel Lucas' eyes set on me again.

We had finished our roast and polished off the pavlova Sam insisted she'd made, but which I suspected she'd bought. I didn't see a Mixmaster in her kitchen and doubted she would have had the strength to beat the eggs with a hand mixer for more than two minutes. Her arms were thick, but not with muscle.

It was nearing ten when Lucas said he had to get home as he had an early start in the morning. I left too. We walked out to the front porch together, and while I searched for something to say, he beat me to it.

'Would you like a ride home?'

The night was calm, and the warm air silky on my shoulders. 'I think I'll walk tonight.'

'Okay. Good night.'

I could sense his disappointment, and it pained me to know I was hurting him, but my mind was somewhere else. Once Lucas had turned the corner, I grabbed at my phone and texted Jack.

You home?

I had worked out Jack wasn't one for communicating through the phone, but I hoped he would reply anyway. All the time I'd spent with him stemmed from him turning up at my house, or meeting at the pub, or him waiting for me outside his house, or me crashing into his vehicle.

But to my surprise, he texted back immediately.

Yeah. Come on over.

When I arrived, his front door was propped open with the flyscreen shut. Music blared from the back of the house. I tapped the door, but he didn't come out. I tried to peer into the living room, but I couldn't see him. I opened the door and stepped inside.

'Hellooo?' My voice barely rivalled the volume of the rock music. 'Hello?'

I took off my heels and closed the door, walked pass his bedroom, bathroom, and kitchen and towards the back of the house to the gym.

Jack was on lying on his back, wearing only gym shorts. I stood in the doorway, watching his bicep curls. His squinted, nose crunched up, and drew a deep breath, grunting as he finished his last one. The weight thumped to the ground and rolled twice as he stretched his arms and peered over to me.

'Three hundred.'

I smiled. 'Sure.'

He smiled back. 'How long have you been standing there?'

'Long enough to be impressed.'

He grabbed the towel by his feet and wiped the sweat from his forehead.

'I let myself in.'

He turned off the music, squirted a stream of water into his mouth from a bottle, then wiped the sweat from his chest. I stood quietly, leaning against the doorway, admiring every perfect inch of his physique. There was not an ounce of fat on his entire body. His black tattoos were a mixture of flora, abstract designs and foreign writing.

'Thirsty?'

'Maybe a water.'

We headed to the kitchen where he poured me a glass of cold water, then sat beside me, resting his elbows on the table.

'What's going on?' he was slowly regaining his breath and his flushed face had started to return to its normal colour.

'I was at Sam's,' I said. 'I was just leaving and didn't really want to go back to the house.' Was he going to tell me I shouldn't have texted? That I was getting too close? That he didn't want a relationship? 'Did you go have your nightly scotch?'

'Sometimes a workout's all I need to clear my head,' he said. 'If it's not enough, I hit the scotch.'

'Why don't you have your nightcap at home?'

'Sometimes I just need a distraction.'

'Am I a distraction?'

He didn't answer. 'So, what brings you here?'

'You,' I paused. 'I was worried you didn't want me to text, I just, wanted to see you I guess.'

'Can't stop thinking about me?' He threw his arms up in an exaggerated stretch. 'Just don't go falling in love. It's a big ask though, I know.'

'I'm surprised your big head fits through the doorways,' I joked. 'And I don't have enough time in Rockford to fall in love with you. Don't you worry your pretty little head. We're having fun, right?'

I stood, then sat on his lap. He set his water bottle down, moved his chair to make more room for the both of us, then ran his hand across my leg, stopping at my thigh. I fixated on his beautiful blue eyes. He kissed the nape of my neck, my lips. We stood and he pulled me towards his bedroom.

I lay on his bed, reminding myself that we were having fun. That it had been a long time since I'd done anything just for fun. That I owed it to myself.

Seventeen

I was getting used to waking up with Jack. Every night that week, after tea, I'd walk over and we'd fall into our routine. We didn't discuss anything of meaning. He would occasionally tell me things that would allude to his childhood – like the fact he'd had a pet dog when he was younger, or that he didn't get good grades in school. He'd talk about some of the antics he got up to when he was a teenager, and I got the sense he'd been popular, but ill-behaved. He'd drunk a lot, copped several traffic fines, and hadn't got home until the early hours. I wondered if he'd had a curfew, or what his parents were like. Jack said he hadn't spoken to his mum for a while. I never asked how long 'a while' meant. And he never mentioned his dad. I didn't ask why. I wanted to ask why. I wanted to ask a lot of questions, but Jack would clam up or change the subject, a lot.

After a week of consecutive sleep-overs with Jack rushing off to work each morning, I woke to find him holding two cups of coffee, one black and one with milk. 'Good morning.'

'Good morning,' I said. 'You haven't showered yet. You're not working today?'

He passed me the coffee and sat down next to me. 'Luckily, no. I'm on days off. What're your plans?'

I rested my head on his warm chest and let my fingers slide to his scar. 'I thought we've been through this before. I live at my parents' house, I'm unemployed and have only a handful of friends. So nothing's on the agenda.'

He ran his hands through my hair and lowered his lips to the top of my head. 'Well, why don't we take a road trip somewhere and get out of here for the day?'

I raised my head. 'Really?'

'You sound surprised.'

'What happened to the warnings of not getting to close, or serious, or falling in love?'

'I didn't ask you to elope. I asked if you wanted to go for a road trip.' He grinned. 'We're just having fun, right?'

I shuffled my bum until I was sitting up against the headboard, the blanket draped over my chest. 'Right.'

'So?'

'So, okay,' I bit my bottom lip. 'Let's go.'

I returned home and quickly went up the stairs without copping a grilling from mum and dad, who were eating breakfast at the kitchen table. Not once during the past week had they asked me where I had been staying, though I think mum knew.

Once I had showered and changed, I skipped down the stairs, my handbag slung over my shoulder and my sunnies balancing on my head.

'See you all later,' I said to the table of inquisitive eyes.

'Where are you off to?' Mum asked and Dad shot her a look as if she had overstepped the boundaries of acceptable questions to a thirty-two-year-old daughter.

'Not sure, just going to go for a road trip.'

'With the neighbour?'

Dad put his paper down and suddenly looked as curious as Mum. If not, a bit concerned.

'Jack?' I said. 'Yes.'

Jimmy looked at Mum and Dad, then turned to me and made a face. The same face he used to make before we got in trouble when we misbehaved or brought home a bad school report.

'Is there a problem?'

'No,' Mum stiffened. 'No, no problem Ruby. No problem, at all.'

'Good.' I headed to the front door but turned back when Mum continued.

'We haven't...' Mum looked at Dad for approval and he nodded, as though they had rehearsed the upcoming lines. 'We haven't heard nice things about him. That he's a bit of a strange character, and has a bit of a... a bit of a...'

'A?'

'A history, Ruby. He's been in trouble with the law,' Dad said. 'He's not the kind of guy you want to be associated with.'

I stepped closer. 'He's not the kind of guy I want to be associated with? And who is? Lucas?'

'We didn't say that,' Mum said.

'As a matter of fact,' Dad interrupted. 'Lucas is the kind of guy you want to be associated with. He's smart, determined, and career-orientated.'

'Rich? Is that the word you're looking for?'

'Now, Ruby,' Mum snapped.

'No, I didn't say that,' Dad continued. 'And I am not saying you should get in a relationship with Lucas again. I am saying he's the kind of guy you should associate yourself with. Not that strange neighbour who's covered in tattoos, doesn't smile at anyone and has a bad reputation.'

I looked out the door window to see if Jack was waiting outside. Not yet.

'So, like, a few parking tickets? Driving without a licence? Break and enter? Murder?' I laughed in disgust. Mum had probably heard he was a loner, so was worried about how it looked to the rest of Rockford – her daughter, the one who was already embroiled in a scandal, spending time with a troubled introvert. 'Is this a bit of a beat up?'

'No,' Dad said. 'It's serious. I know a lot of people in the business, Ruby. I've asked around. They said he's known to the police.'

'So, you've done your homework then Dad? You've been spying?'

'No.' He got up and walked to me, placing a hand on my shoulder. 'I wouldn't spy on my daughter. But I work with criminals every day…'

'Criminal?' I shrugged my shoulder and he pulled away. 'We don't even know what he's done. And if he has a bit of a history, like you say he does, it's history. I have a history, you have a history, we all have a history.'

Dad looked back at Mum, who was tapping her toes. Jimmy remained still, watching the show play out around him.

'I can look into it further. I would just suggest until we know the facts that you stop spending time with him. And think about how Michelle would cope if the tabloids got hold of this information.'

'They won't get a hold of this information. There's been nobody following me, pestering me or butting into my business in Rockford. Until now. Stay out of it.'

'We want to protect you, Ruby,' Mum said softly.

'I don't need protection,' I shot. 'I need to be able to do what I want to do for once. To make my own decisions.' I softened my voice. 'Just for the next month, please.'

'I think we need to re-evaluate that too,' Mum said. 'Three months is just not long enough of a break…'

'Don't pressure her,' Dad raised his voice and held up his hand. Jimmy picked up the newspaper and began reading again, as though the start of an argument between Mum and Dad signified the end of the show.

'I'm not pressuring her,' she snapped. 'It's just a suggestion.'

Jack's ute started up in his driveway. I opened the door and cleared my throat, taking a deep breath in hopes of curbing my anger. 'Please, don't worry.' My voice shook and my toe tapped. 'I have a clear head. I can make clear decisions. I'll be okay.'

Dad looked to the floor and scratched the back of his neck. Mum bit her shaking lip to stop herself saying more.

'Really,' I said reassuringly, then shut the door behind me.

I climbed into Jack's vehicle. He leaned over in his tidy blue button-up shirt, which made his eyes pop, and kissed me. His chin was smooth and his subtle cologne swept through my nose and into my stomach, sending off a surge of butterflies. He grabbed my hand and reversed with the other.

'Where are we going?'

'I thought we could just go for a drive and see where the road takes us.'

'I like that idea.'

We drove for about half an hour through roads I hadn't seen for years. Past apple orchards and dense vineyards, green parks and yellow fields, all the while digging up memories planted in my younger years. We turned down a backroad and a cloud of dust swept over the windshield, the same way it had that day back in Sam's cousin's car.

It was during our second-last year of school. I had been trying to swallow a breath of fresh air through the partially-opened window but instead coughed on the mixture of loose earth and rolled herb that Sam, her cousin and his friend were passing between them. I was anxious, unsure of where we were going. I told Sam's cousin I needed to go home, I had class with an acting coach that evening. But, with a broken laugh and hazy eyes, he refused.

'Take it easy,' Sam said. 'You need to learn to have fun once in a while. Let go of the rules.'

We started a bonfire surrounded by a grove of trees and we drank and danced to music from the stereo in the back of the car. I tried to relax but couldn't help checking my watch and glancing at the car.

About thirty more people showed up, all older than Sam and I. The girls –students who hadn't yet returned to uni after the summer holidays – looked down on us, as if we were children. I studied their clothes, their hair, their movements, while Sam studied the men. She disappeared several times with different groups, returning more dry-eyed and dopey than the time before, until eventually her legs couldn't move and her face froze.

I called Lucas to pick us up, and though he never said it, I knew he was disappointed in me for skipping acting class again, for hanging out with a crowd I didn't know and for trusting in my stoned friend. After we dropped Sam off, he refused to look at me, and when I asked if he wanted to hang out the following day, he flatly refused.

He wasn't always incredibly responsible. I'd seen him stumble into rose bushes after too many beers and polish off a bag of chips after a joint with Jimmy, but he was always the voice of reason. 'There's a time and a place,' he would say. 'We have to have our priorities in order.'

He would shake his head at Sam's behaviour and tell me that she was throwing her life away, that she was an embarrassment to herself.

'I'm not Sam,' I used to say. 'I won't be wasted potential.'

While Jack drove past old tin sheds, blue reservoirs and abandoned cars, I recalled playing with old school friends at their parents' farms, swimming in dams on pumped up tyres, family car rides to fetes and fairs. I was lost so deep in the memories that I hadn't recognised the silence between Jack and I. He hadn't said a word to interrupt my train of thought, but when I felt his gaze sway from the road and fall on me, I turned to see his signature semi-smile.

'Turn left here,' I demanded after spotting a sign: Hedley Waterfalls, 200m ahead. 'I forgot about this place! Dad and Mum used to bring Jimmy and I out here when we were young. We'd put on our bathers and play under the waterfalls and Mum would always pack a picnic. I hope it's as good as I remembered.'

Jack turned and drove down a small windy road until we hit an empty car park. I opened my door and motioned to him. 'C'mon.'

I followed the picket signs towards the falls with Jack close behind. The only glimpse of sunshine ducked behind heavy grey clouds. The breeze was slight, but I predicated the rain wasn't far away. I zipped up my black hooded jumper and held my hands out as I navigated the rocky path.

We walked for about half a kilometre with only the sound of birds chirping and the waterfalls in the background.

'I think we're getting close.'

The roar of the tumbling water got louder.

Jack took a few quick steps until he was at my side. He put his hand on my back as we emerged from the narrow trail into a beautiful, open gorge. It was exactly how I remembered it, except the clear blue water was tinted a pale grey by the overhead clouds.

'Well, this is it,' I said, stretching out my arms. 'This is where I often used to spend Sundays with the Johns clan.'

Jack put one foot up on a loose boulder, and tucked his hands in his pockets. 'Must be nice to think about.'

He was fixated on the falls and I couldn't tell if he was captivated by their beauty or lost in thought.

'Yeah,' I said. 'I guess. One of the things that's exactly as I remember. One nice memory in my otherwise messed-up life.'

'You almost sound convincing.' He sat on a boulder, his eyes still on the falls.

I sat next to him, rubbing my elbow against his. 'You don't believe my life's a mess?'

'Is it?' He looked to me. 'You seem like you've got it all. Wealthy parents, a successful career, a brother, a best friend.'

'Is that what it takes to qualify for a happy life?'

'I wouldn't know.'

I tried to study his pupils and the curve of his lip. Neither faltered. I took a deep breath.

'Well, maybe if you picked up the entertainment section of the paper, or flipped through a magazine once awhile, you would know that my life isn't picture perfect.'

'I don't always trust what I read in those magazines.'

That's a relief. If only more people were like Jack and didn't believe everything they read. There's always more to the story.

I didn't say anything.

'So, what would I read then?' he asked. 'What would I read about you?'

I thought about it for a second, whether I should let him in, whether it would be too deep for him, whether it would scare him away. But maybe if I told him more about my past, he'd reciprocate.

'They would probably say Anna Johns – the overdose. Or Anna Johns – her secret life. Or Anna Johns – her hideaway.' I swallowed and whispered, 'Or Anna Johns – a broken woman.'

I closed my mouth, looked at the ring on my index finger and waited.

'You just don't look like an Anna.'

I sighed. 'That's it?'

He lifted his shoulders. 'What?'

'No follow-up questions?'

'If you want to tell me, you will.' He raised his knees and wrapped his arms around them.

After a few seconds of silence, I continued. 'It was an accident. The overdose. I got carried away at work. I took on too much and struggled to keep up with my demanding schedule. I was only a couple of months into filming a 1960s comedy, and I was cast to play a go-go girl. That day, on set, I was expected to get through a ten-hour day. This was after a two-hour gym session, three television interviews, a meeting with my acting coach and a magazine photo shoot. I took a Xanax before I went to bed, but woke up in a fog. I was so exhausted it took me about fifteen minutes before I mustered up enough energy to roll over and turn off my alarm.

'One of the guys on set noticed me yawning heaps and told me he could help. He gave me some Adderall and told me if I wanted a quick jolt to snort them, but I said I wasn't into that sort of thing.'

'But you did?'

'Desperation won.'

I didn't tell Jack everything. I didn't tell him how my head was a blur as I sat in the make-up chair, trying to retain everything Michelle was rambling on about. How she was sitting next to me, giving strict instructions about the scene ahead and the scheduled meetings that followed. I didn't tell him how, five minutes before I was meant to be on set, I went back to my caravan, closed the curtains and desperately emptied the contents of my handbag onto a table and retrieved the bottle of pills.

I remember struggling to pop the lid, pouring the lot onto the table, crushing them with the bottom of a water glass, rolling up a five-dollar note and snorting the pile of powder.

I shook my face and grabbed at my nostrils, trying to stop the nagging tickle. I sat on the floor awaiting a buzz, closed my eyes, and nearly didn't open them again.

'A fast fix almost cost me my life.'

He stared at me. Was he concerned? Or did he just think less of me?

'Stupid. I know,' I continued. 'The stupidest thing I have done in my life, really. But I'm not an addict. Though I think my parents think otherwise. If they should worry about anyone, it's themselves.'

'Yeah?'

I knew I was rambling, but I couldn't stop. It was like the flood gates had opened and I was releasing the weight of the ocean onto Jack.

'Yeah. Dad and Mum are a mess. They've apparently been fighting for years, which shouldn't have surprised me, really. Dad's got another life on the side, Mum's too busy trying to convince everyone they're fine. Meanwhile, their grown son is living in their house, high as a kite, probably unable to function without his weed, and he's washing dishes at my friend's pub.' I silently laughed to myself. 'Now their grown daughter is living at home with them too. We're all winning at life, aren't we?' A few staggered drops of light rain fell onto my face and arms.

He looked me up and down. 'So, a go-go girl.'

I smiled. 'Is that all you took from that information overload?'

'I'm trying to paint a picture.'

'Yes, a go-go girl. I'll have you know I've been a single mother, a struggling author, an abusive teacher, a sexy secretary, a teenage waitress. I've played every part.'

'You must be a good actress if you had everyone fooled.'

I nodded. 'I guess.'

His face turned serious. 'Life's a game sometime, Ruby. We can play by the rules or make up our own. It doesn't really matter. We all end up in the same place.' He looked at the sky. 'Should we head back?'

I shook my head. 'We only just got here.' I stood, grabbed his hand and pulled him up to me. 'If life's a game, let's play up.'

I walked towards the gorge and leaped onto a partially submerged boulder. The raindrops created wavering rings in the water. I hopped from one rock to another, careful not to lose my footing. Jack made it look a lot easier, taking large strides across the top of the boulders beside me. We made our way towards the plunging falls and stopped at a patch of grass dampened by the falls' spray and the light rain. I closed my eyes and breathed in the smell of fresh water and wet grass. It was a gentle, welcoming scent – the kind I'd longed for among the heavily polluted, food truck-riddled New York roads. Jack took off his hoodie and placed it down for me to sit on, then wrapped his arm around me as I nestled in.

'Looks inviting.'

I pulled away from Jacks and looked to him. 'The water?' I asked.

He nodded and stripped off his top.

'You're serious?'

He stood, unbuckled his belt, unzipped the fly of his jeans and dropped them around his waist, exposing his white briefs. 'Very serious.' He kicked off his shoes and put his hand out to me. 'You coming?'

'Nope.' I laughed.

'Suit yourself.'

I watched as he disappeared into a steep trail behind me. I stood and tried to get a glimpse of him. I waited for almost a minute until he appeared at a cliff near the top of the falls.

'You can't jump,' I yelled. 'I don't know how deep it is along that edge.'

He threw his hands up, waved at me, and my heart raced in fear.

'Who taught me to take a gamble?'

I watched as he flung himself forward. His face lit up with pure exuberance and my heart plunged with him as he sunk into the water below. My toes tapped uncontrollably until he emerged a few seconds later. I gasped, unaware that I hadn't inhaled for seconds. Jack shook his head, wiped his eyes and burst into a laughter.

'You are crazy!'

'Whatcha waiting for? Come on in. Didn't you just say something about playing up for a bit?' He treaded the water, focused on me, his grin unbroken.

I heard Sam's youthful voice inside my mind. 'You need to learn to have fun once in a while. Let go of the rules.'

'Okay,' I muttered. 'Okay, okay.'

He threw his fist in the air. 'Yes!'

I took off my clothes, leaving on only the matching black bra and undies I had chosen on the assumption Jack would see them at the end of the date, not in the middle.

I walked up the steep hill, following the footsteps Jack had made in the dirt only moments prior. A wave of energy rushed from my toes to my fingertips when I reached the top. Jack waited in the water below, looking up with anticipation. At that moment, there was no-one to hide from. No strangers, no lurking cameras, just Jack. And there was nothing left for me to keep from him. He knew it all.

I took off my bra and undies and threw them to the ground below, narrowly missing our pile of clothes. I was both physically and mentally stripped bare.

There I stood, naked at the top of the cliff with my skin gently kissed by the cool air and faint drops from the darkening sky. Jack's enthusiastic grin softened. His lips parted and he smiled with a sort of pride, or lust, or both. I liked it. I felt at ease. Invigorated, almost.

'You're not scared, are you?' he yelled.

I jumped forward, a rush surging through me as I fell. The cold water slapped my skin, and I blew out through my nose as I sank. The surface rippled above. I closed my eyes and let the rollercoaster of emotions disappear. When I finally felt calm, and a little bit of pride, I swam to the top to see Jack paddling towards me.

'How was that?'

'I can't believe I did that!'

'I can't either. I didn't think you would.' He kissed my forehead, then kissed my lips. I grasped his waist to hold myself up, and he kicked his feet to keep us afloat. We swam until we could stand on the rocky sand in the shallows.

'Something tells me you love adrenaline.'

He smiled. 'I used to.'

I wanted more. 'How did your parents handle an adrenaline junkie?'

He threw his arms over his head then shook them in the water. 'Dad never got to see that part of me. He walked out when I was young.'

'I'm sorry.'

His smiled faded. 'He took me to footy practice when I was nine. Somewhere between 8 am and 9 am that Saturday, he disappeared. My coach waited around after practice, but after a few hours, called my mum and told her the news.'

I touched his face. 'And that's it?'

'That was it. That was the last I saw of Dad.'

I pried further. 'How was your mum?'

'Not surprised. Said he'd packed up most of his valuables months before and shipped them somewhere. Not sure where. Left her to raise me on her own, pay for our mortgage on her own, pay for her car, which she had to sell.' Jack paused and I thought he was going to change the subject again. But he continued. 'She worked about four different jobs to keep us going. I tried to help when I got older, but I could have done it a lot better.'

It was the most Jack had spoken about himself. And he spoke about such tragic circumstances as if they were ordinary. I wanted to ask more, but the rain was coming down hard and fast now, the combination of thick droplets and dense wind stinging our cheeks. Goosebumps spread over my neck and shoulders.

We grabbed our clothes which were already drenched from the downpour and ran towards the carpark, hunched over.

We were nearly at the end of the trail when I heard footsteps and loud whispers coming towards us. I looked up to see two Asian tourists in bright yellow ponchos, holding umbrellas. They stopped in their tracks when they saw our naked bodies. The woman, aged in her mid-twenties, threw a hand over her mouth, struggling to keep the umbrella over her head in the heavy wind. The man, who I assumed was her boyfriend or husband, was only a couple feet behind.

He grabbed his camera from around his neck with his free hand and lifted it.

'No, no, no!' I shook one of my hands at him and scrambled to hide myself with the pile of wet clothes. 'No! No pictures please!'

Jack put his hand on my back and pushed me forward. 'Nothing to see here.'

We ran to his ute, dripping head to toe in water and howling with laughter. My stomach ached and tears poured from my eyes, mixing with the rain running from my wet hair down my cheeks. Jack thrust his head back and snorted between laughs.

'Wow,' I managed between fits. 'I can't believe that. He was going to take a picture!'

Jack started the engine and turned up the heat. He dug under his seat and passed me one of his oversized jumpers.

'Put this on for now,' he said.

'What will you wear?'

He slipped off his briefs and set them on the wet pile of clothes at my feet. 'Nothing at all.'

EIGHTEEN

I wrapped myself in a blanket and got cosy on Jack's couch while he made us sandwiches in his kitchen. Rain thumped against the window and roof. I grabbed the remote and flipped through television shows until my face appeared on screen.

I was playing the part of a quiet farm girl who fell in love with a high-profile businessman and moved to the city to live a luxurious life. The film had almost made the top ten highest-grossing movies in the box office that month, and it was the last movie I made before I felt the weight of the world on my shoulders.

Acting was easy. It came natural to me. The difficulties had lain beyond that. With each success came more diet plans, more gym sessions, more meetings and much less sleep. When Michelle saw my work slipping, my mood shifting and suspected something was wrong, she recommended that I talk to someone, a counsellor. I refused, which I hadn't often done. It would have only meant one more meeting to squeeze into my already hectic schedule.

'That's you.' Jack put a plate of sandwiches down, an assortment of tuna and ham, cut into small triangles. I grabbed a tuna one.

'Yup,' I said with a mouthful, flicking the channel back to music.

He grabbed the remote and flicked it back. 'I actually know this movie.'

'I thought you never watched movies?'

'Rarely. Is that really you?'

'Yup.' I tried to take the remote from him, but he held it over his head. 'Let's turn this off.'

'You look so young.'

'Thanks a lot.' I settled back into my seat and took another bite.

'How old is this movie?'

'Only five years. I was twenty-seven. The last few years has taken a toll on me.'

He peered at me with squinted eyes, dropped the remote on the table and grabbed a sandwich. 'You look good now, too. Not a day over thirty-two.'

I slapped him gently and giggled, careful not to spit any crumbs out. 'C'mon now. Be nice.'

I felt awkward watching myself, but I couldn't look at Jack. I was used to criticism, but couldn't bare it coming from him. For the past two weeks, I hadn't brought myself to look for my name onscreen or in ink, so the last thing I wanted to read was a critique written all over his face. Instead I stared at the cobwebs that hung from the ceiling, at the bits of fluff on his quilt, at

A PLAN UNRAVELLED

the dust on the coffee table. Jack lifted his feet and crossed them on the table beside the sandwich plate, and I traced my eyes along his stretched-out legs, his black t-shirt, which clung to his torso, and up to his face. He was staring at me.

'What?' I said.

'You're really talented.'

'Thank you,' I whispered.

'Why are you here?'

'What do you mean?' I sat up straight and fidgeted my hands. 'At your house?'

'In Rockford?'

'Honestly?' My body tensed, and I tried to stretch my back, but failed to loosen up. I took a deep breath. If I wanted to know his story, I had better show him the same respect. I swallowed and shifted in my seat. 'After the overdose, my publicist told me to get out of New York while she handled damage control. I wanted to go somewhere a lot nicer, where I could sip cocktails or relax in a private pool, but I've been heavy-handed with my spending, so this was the only option.'

Jack muted the movie. 'Doesn't every second person in the movie business have an overdose? It's nothing new, is it? And yours was purely accidental.'

'I think that's why the tabloids had a heyday. It was unexpected coming from me. And instead of caring if I was hurt or okay, they just wanted to dig up more dirt. Anything they could get their hands on. They wanted to paint a new picture of me. So Michelle threw her hands in the air and told me to get out of town. Hide away for a bit.'

Jack bit his lip and scratched the back of his neck.

'So that's why I'm here. I lost control.'

He nodded slowly.

'I think I overstepped our boundaries?' I said softly, hoping to lighten the mood. 'We're supposed to be keeping things light and fun, right?'

He ignored the question. 'Do you miss it?'

'I miss working.'

'Do you miss New York?'

The rain had stopped. The sun shifted from behind the clouds filling the room with its warm light. A single bird chirped from the front lawn, breaking the silence between us.

I grabbed Jack's hand, thought about his questions, shook my head and kissed him.

Nineteen

April

The green leaves had changed to red and a cool breeze had settled into the evenings.

I watched Ron mow the neighbour's lawn. Even from the kitchen window, I could see the dark circles under his eyes and that the skin on his face didn't cling as it once had. He glanced over occasionally while pushing back and forth. I waved once, but he didn't seem to see me through the half-open blinds. Now he was pushing the mower back into the garage.

It was nearly 5 pm and the house was filled with the smell of bolognaise and cheese sauce as a lasagne baked in the oven. Bags of lettuce, carrots, tomatoes and mushrooms sat on the bench nearby.

'What are you watching?' Mum sprung up behind me and peered over my shoulder to see Ron getting into his car. She grabbed a corkscrew then a bottle of red from a wine rack above the fridge, her mood visibly shifting as she popped the cork. She poured herself a glass, nearly spilling it over the rim. 'Honestly, Ruby. Some people need to know when to move on in life, don't they?'

'I doubt he needs the money, Mum. I think he must garden because he likes it and wants to keep busy.'

She tore open the bag of carrots and grabbed the two largest, waving them in front of me like she was shaking a wand. 'Maybe, maybe not. Some people need to know when to leave the past in the past.' She rapidly cut the carrots into thin pieces, breathing heavy as she did. Shreds flung from the knife and onto her freshly swept floor. 'How can anyone have a future if they're stuck in old habits? Grab some dressing, will you?'

Mum shred the lettuce with her hands as I grabbed balsamic vinegar from the fridge. 'Maybe we're all a bit like Ron. You always said there's comfort in the familiar.'

Mum snatched the dressing, poured it over the lettuce, and tossed the salad with two large spoons until each leaf had been coated several times over.

'Mum?'

She didn't look up.

'Mum?'

'What is it, Ruby?' She wiped her brow with her forearm and pushed back the loose bits of grey-speckled hair that hung in her face. When it dropped back over her eyes, she blew a gust of air from the side of her mouth, causing the strand to loop and cling to her cheek.

'I think the salad's ready.'

She stared into the bowl.

'Is everything okay? What's going on?'

Before she could answer, Dad's car pulled past Ron's outside and roared into the driveway. I suspected Mum knew about Dad's tryst, but of course it was one of those subjects we never discussed. She couldn't look weak in front of her children. She lifted her shoulders, straightened her shirt and placed the salad bowl on the table.

'Set the table for one more tonight.' Dad demanded as he hung his black overcoat in the entry closet and untied his scarf and wrapped it around the hanger. 'I invited a guest.'

'I wish you would have told me, all I made is lasagne.' Mum's agitation returned.

'Don't stress. Lasagne is perfect.' He poured himself a glass of wine and leaned against the kitchen bench. 'It's quite casual.'

'Well, who is it?' Mum reached for the dinner setting from the overhead cabinets. She only brought out those plates, rimmed with a gold lining, and matching gold-plated cutlery, when we had guests. She received them as a fiftieth birthday present and they still sparkled like they did when she took them out of the package nine years prior.

'Lucas Rogers.'

My heart sunk, but I forced a smile when Mum looked to me with her wide eyes and open mouth.

'Mark,' she whispered loudly. 'Maybe you should have asked Ruby first.'

'Uh, no. That's fine. We're friends,' I said. At least, I still hoped.

'Good, then it's sorted. I thought it would be nice for Lucas to come around and spend some time with us. Then I can have a casual chat to him about joining the firm. He's expressed interest. I thought I'd see what the kid has to offer.'

My hands formed a fist and my toe began to tap. Lucas had never told me he wanted to work with Dad, and my mind raced as to why. I was under the impression he was doing well at his firm, that he was content in his life after his whirlwind marriage and city escape. I'd thought he genuinely wanted to get close to me because he still loved me, but now I questioned his motives.

'He's not a kid anymore,' Mum said, setting the table.

Dad rolled his eyes. 'Obviously. But he was a good kid. Smart, funny, kind. A real genuine bloke. The sort I would want in the firm or in the family, for that matter.'

'Now, Mark!' Mum shouted. 'We already fought about this once…'

'Mum, it's okay—'

'No, Ruby. It's not. You already expressed your disappointment with us the other day. We're not trying to meddle. We know you are a grown woman with—'

Dad slammed his glass on the kitchen bench. Tiny droplets of red spilled over the top and splashed onto his wrist.

I handed him a tea towel.

'Dammit, I was just cracking a joke. I don't mean anything by it. I invited Lucas over, not for Ruby, but for my own intentions.'

'Well, that I can believe.'

Dad mumbled. 'What in the hell is that supposed to mean?'

'It means you are selfish, Mark. You are selfish!' Mum's voice was loud and abrupt.

Jimmy emerged from his room looking, and smelling, like he had rolled around in a puddle of cologne. 'Damn, you guys are embarrassing sometimes.'

'We are embarrassing?' Dad lifted his head, still raging. 'Get yourself a real job and move out of this damn house, already. You're nearly thirty. Who's the embarrassing one now?'

'That's unnecessary,' Mum muttered under her breath as she stabbed the lasagne and quickly dragged the knife to form slices.

'Unnecessary? It's the truth, dammit.' He laughed. 'It's an embarrassment to me, when I have to explain to people that my children, my very capable, adult children, are still living at home.'

Jimmy sat at the table, scratching his head and I drew in a breath. I had no defence. I was embarrassed, too. I was embarrassed that I had, only months ago, had everything at my fingertips. I had a promising future. And then I blew it.

A heavy knock echoed from the front door, breaking the tension.

Lucas stepped in and shook Dad's hand. There was a slight tremble in his otherwise steady composure. His hair curled in perfect ringlets and his eyes were big with trepidation.

'Nice to see you again, Lucas,' Mum kissed his cheek.

'You too, Mrs Johns.' He handed over his coat. He was dressed professionally, in black slacks and a grey, fitted button-up shirt. It was a lot looser than it would have been on Jack. A few chest hairs peeped over his opened top button. 'Hi, Jimmy. Hi, Ruby.'

'Can I get you a glass of red,' Mum asked, 'or white? Or anything?'

'I'll have a glass of red please.' He kept his eyes on me as he followed Mum to the kitchen bench. 'Beautiful. It's smells beautiful.'

'It's just lasagne. I hope you don't mind.'

'If I remember correctly, you make an amazing lasagne,' he said.

'Well, let's hope it's as good as you remember.' She handed us both a glass.

'I'm sure it will measure up.' He winked at me. I folded my arms across my chest and bit my bottom lip. My heart thumped. I wanted to take Lucas aside and ask if he was using me. But I didn't want to cause a scene. I didn't want to look jealous. So, I put on my acting hat and returned a smile. I reminded myself to breath slowly and steady my fluttering toes.

I sat across from Lucas, who answered Mum's questions about his work and Melbourne. I winced every time she brought up a memory, but Lucas didn't seem to mind.

'Lucas, remember when you accidently locked yourself in our bathroom for over an hour?' She laughed. 'We all thought you had gone home without saying anything until you finally decided to bang on the door and we heard you over Jimmy's music.

'Remember when you slipped on our driveway and got that huge bruise on your face? Oh, I felt terrible for you. Right before school pictures.

'Remember when you and Ruby were watching that horror movie and you screamed so loud you woke up Mark?'

For a moment, I forgot I was angry and laughed so hard I had to throw my hand over my mouth to hide the escaping crumbs.

'I remember,' he said, tapping the table while trying to catch his breath between laughs.

I'd forgotten how he would tap his hand on the table or his knee when he laughed heartily or how he slicked his hair back off his face when he tried to calm himself. I forgot how he picked at his food with his fork several times before taking a bite and how well he got on with my parents. I forgot how easy it was for him to speak about almost anything or everything, with anyone.

Lucas wiped his mouth, pushed his plate back and ran his hands over his hair. 'Just as I remembered, amazing.'

Mum blushed 'Thank you.'

'Lucas, have you thought about my request? I think we could come up with a bit of a deal.' Dad coughed.

'I have thought about it and I would be interested in hearing more, sir.'

'Sir.' Dad pointed his finger. 'You were always a man with great respect. I knew you would do well for yourself.'

'Thank you,' Lucas said with a hint of modesty.

'Maybe you guys can give us some time to ourselves to talk business.'

'Of course, dear.' Mum stood and straightened her shirt. 'I'll just get you some apple crumble.'

I followed her to the kitchen bench.

'Are you okay?' Mum whispered.

'Everything's fine.'

A PLAN UNRAVELLED

'Does he know about Jack?' She slipped ice cream onto the desserts. She had moved in close and waited for an answer.

'Jack and I aren't serious. Lucas and I are friends. We're fine.' I felt the same uncertainty as I did when I was unsatisfied with an acting performance. I could hear the director inside my head yelling at me to be more convincing.

'I told you I don't want to pry, and I respect your decision, but he still loves you.' With two plates in her hand, she leaned forward to whisper in my ear again. 'He looks at you the same way he did when he was young.' She walked past me and set the plates in front of Lucas and Dad, who didn't pause from conversation. She reached over them, grabbed the bottle of red and tipped the remainder in their glasses.

Mum and I retreated to the living room and watched television for more than an hour until we heard the kitchen chairs scrape across the floor. Mum motioned for me to come with her to the front door, where Dad and Lucas stood, laughing about something.

'You're leaving?' Mum asked.

'Yes. Thank you for tea. It was beautiful.'

'I look forward to speaking to you in a couple days,' Dad said, shaking Lucas's hand. 'I hope you can follow through.'

'I won't let you down, sir,' Lucas said, avoiding any eye contact with me.

'I just want a positive outcome for everyone.' Dad said slowly.

'I understand, sir.'

I closed the door for him and waved through the window as he walked towards his car on the street. But as Dad and Mum receded to the living room, I went out after him.

'Hey.'

He turned to me.

'When were you going to tell me you were after a job with my dad?'

He spun his keys in his finger, closed the car door and leaned against it. 'I don't know.'

I stopped a couple feet from him and crossed my arms.

'Should I have?'

'Probably. Considering.'

'Considering what?' He took a step closer to me. 'Considering there's nothing between us? You made that perfectly clear. I would have told you if something, you know, eventuated.'

'You would have?'

'Of course.'

'You would have said, "Hey Ruby, I love that we're back together. By the way, can you put in a good word to your dad for me? I'd like to work with him."'

His forehead scrunched and he threw his hands over his hair. 'Oh, you've got to be kidding me.'

I held my hands to my side. 'No, I'm dead serious.'

A PLAN UNRAVELLED

'You think I am using you? You think I heard you were back in town and thought, Hey, perfect. I can bank on my first love to get me ahead in my career? Are you bloody kidding me?'

I dropped my hands and swallowed the lump in my throat. Lucas stepped closer and lowered his voice.

'I'm real, Ruby. I'm not an actor.' His eyes were set on mine. 'If I had to choose between you or my career, I wouldn't be choosing the latter, I tell you that right now. I've put myself out there. I've never lied to you. I'm pretty sure you can see right through me. You always could. You think I've come up with some elaborate plan?'

I stepped back. 'I don't know. I don't know what to believe.'

'Clearly you don't know me anymore, and I certainly don't know you.' He clutched his keys in his closed fist, got in his car and started the engine. I watched as he disappeared into the distance.

TWENTY

Michelle had forwarded me a few emails she had exchanged with up and coming directors who were interested in working with me when I returned. None sounded appealing.

I looked up from my laptop to see a tanned and glowing Sam prance into my room. She flashed her freshly manicured nails as she held up a brown plastic bag wrapped with a red ribbon.

'I brought you something!'

'Oh, what is it?' I rubbed my hands together and crossed my legs.

'Open it.' She handed me the bag, sat on the bed next to me and leaned in.

I untied the bow and pulled out a silver bracelet with pendant in the shape of half a feather.

'It's a friendship bracelet.' She pulled it from my hands and wrapped it around my wrist. 'I know you should only really wear these when you're like, twelve, but I saw them on our holiday and I couldn't resist. We were too cool for these when we were young, so now's the perfect time.' She clipped the clasp then pulled her sleeve up over her elbow to reveal her half of the set. 'It's not a match for your other jewellery but...'

'What do you mean?'

'You know...it didn't cost a lot of money.' She rolled her eyes. 'But its sentiment is worth more than the cash I paid for it.'

'Thanks, Sam.' I lifted my hand to see both the bracelet and the ring on my index finger. 'It's perfect. You're too sweet.'

'I know!' She took off her white zip-up jumper then lay back, using it as a pillow. She crossed her legs and sighed.

I scanned her hands, but there was no sign of a ring. 'How was it?'

'Amazing! Amazing. I think I fell even more in love. I don't know how he does it, but he is amazing.'

I raised my eyebrows. 'I asked how the trip was, not Harry.'

'I know. It was paradise. But Harry made it exceptional.' She rolled onto her side and swept her long wavy blond strands out of her eyes. 'He organised a breakfast on the beach at sunrise. Then organised two massages, he got strawberries delivered to our room. He's such a romantic.' She then pushed her hand into her pocket and pulled out a beautiful gold diamond ring. 'Then ta-da! This happened!'

She slid it onto her ring finger and I threw my arms around her. 'Congratulations, Sam! That's wonderful!'

'I knew it was going to happen. Now I have to start the planning.'

I held her tight, thinking about how much she had changed. How everything had fallen into place for her. How she worked tirelessly in a small-town pub, had fallen in love with a hardworking tradie, lived modestly, but seemed to have it all.

'I'm happy for you, babe.' I let go and we both lay on my bed, knees bent, staring at the roof. 'First comes love, then comes marriage, then…'

'Don't.' She shot a finger up and laughed. 'Let's not jump the uterus gun. One thing at a time.'

I laughed. 'I could see you and Harry with a bunch of little terrors.'

'Yeah?' She looked at me.

'Of course!'

She smiled and looked back to the ceiling. 'Me too. One day.'

'So, besides wedding planning, what's up for the rest of the week?'

'Work, work and more work,' she moaned. 'What about you? Must be nice living the highlife. Not, you know, literally.'

I blew out air in a vibrating mirth. 'Decisions. Michelle might have some offers for me to consider.'

She rolled over and squealed. 'That's great!'

I huffed. 'Isn't it?'

'Starting over is daunting. Uncertainty is daunting. Life is daunting. But you can sit around and mope, go back to acting, or stay here and do something else. You have the choice, my friend.'

'Stay here and do what?'

'I don't know. Teach people your skills. You can start with the teenyboppers who try to sneak into The Night Owl pretending like they're eighteen. They need some acting lessons.'

I peered towards the window, wondering when I would hear Jack's car in his driveway or the sound of heavy work boots on the path to his front door. I wondered what a permanent life back in Australia would be like. Or who it would be with. Was my Harry in Rockford?

I waited on Jack's doorstep with two noodle boxes from the only Asian shop in Rockford. He answered wearing nothing but blue jeans, his short hair still wet from a shower. My eyes fell on his scar. He'd never tried to conceal it from me, but had never spoken about it either. A five o'clock shadow had formed over his face. I liked the stubble. I handed him the noodles and followed him to the kitchen, where he dished the food into two large bowls and poured us each a glass of red.

He slurped as he shovelled the noodles, as if he hadn't eaten for weeks. I took my time, twirling them around my fork and carefully slipping them into my mouth to avoid any mess.

'What have you been up to?' he asked.

'My friend came around today. The one who owns the pub. Sam's just got back from a holiday with her boyfriend. They got engaged.'

'Oh yeah?'

'She knew it was coming. She kept dropping hints.'

Jack stared into his bowl, slurping up the last of his noodles and spraying his chin with bits of teriyaki sauce. I giggled as I slid my thumb across his chin, wiping away the mess. 'You should hang out with us sometime.'

He didn't answer.

I pushed my bowl aside. 'I don't think I can eat anymore.'

'Me neither.' He stood and walked to the sink, carrying both our bowls. I followed, wrapped my arms around his waist and kissed him on the back of his neck. He grabbed my hands and turned around, kissing me gently, his nose against mine and his eyelashes brushing my eyelids. As we stood in his dingy kitchen with dirty dishes in the sink and crumbs of Jack's breakfast spread on the bench, breathing in the lingering smell of noodles, I thought about Sam. Maybe she was onto something. Starting over was hard, whether it be in New York or in Rockford. I had to sort out what I wanted, and maybe I'd come to a point where the things I once wanted, didn't matter anymore. The apartment, the money, the fame that came from a life-sucking career. All of which was never enough to meet the unachievable expectations of

A PLAN UNRAVELLED

Michelle, of prominent players in the movie industry and, most importantly, of myself.

Maybe all I needed to be happy was wrapped in my arms, kissing me in that dingy kitchen.

TWENTY-ONE

Mum rocked side to side, singing along to her golden oldies, tapping her fingers on the steering wheel and staring ahead through her oversized sunnies. I hadn't seen her face glow like that since my last movie premier. She was a stark contrast to the woman who'd picked me up from the hospital ten weeks prior.

I rested my elbow on the door, peering out the window at the vast countryside. The cows, the birds, the openness of the sky, unshielded by buildings or billboards. The grass was bright green from the recent rain. The roads were strewn with pot holes formed from the passing semi's and local tractors with their machinery. Along the golden fields, we passed a kookaburra perched on a leaning wooden-fence, a flock of cockatoos and a pair of rosellas. A blue-tongue lizard made a lucky escape between the front and rear tyres of Mum's car, which couldn't be said for the dead wombat and kangaroo on the side of the road, which, going by the state of them, must have been hit days earlier. Mum didn't see me smile at the sight, if so, she would have flashed me a worried look. But I would have been forgiven if I explained the Myna birds and black blow flies that plagued Rockford didn't measure up to the native Australian wildlife I'd been missing since my return.

'Oh, come on Rubes,' Mum said, 'you know the words. Or have you forgotten your Aussie icons?'

Besides classical and opera music, Mum had a weak spot for nineties Aussie bands. I remember helping her to close the blinds, move the couches back, and remove the fresh flowers in the living room before we would spin in circles and belt out tunes to the radio. I didn't pay much notice to when the impromptu dance parties slowed and eventually stopped. Either Mum lost her spontaneity, or I outgrew fun.

I turned up the radio, bopped my head, tapped my knee and joined in. Mum got louder, so I did too. I closed my eyes and was back in that living room, belting out every line, swaying my head, lost in the music. It wasn't until the song was over that I realised Mum had missed the exit to the yoga retreat.

'We're going to Melbourne Mum.' I looked over my shoulder. 'You have to turn around. You missed the exit!'

She winked through her dark lenses and flashed me a smile. 'Oh no I didn't.'

I raised an eyebrow and turned the volume down.

She stared into the distance, her cheeky grin frozen.

'What do you mean?' I asked slowly.

'Honey.' She lowered her sunnies to the tip of her nose and looked at me over them. 'In all these years, me and the girls have been on one yoga retreat.'

I tilted my head, my mouth parted, my eyebrow still raised.

'It was so bloody boring.'

I put my hand over my open mouth.

'Sue suggested we go to Melbourne one year, and it was the best weekend of our lives. We haven't looked back.'

'Mum,' I squealed. 'And you guys keep it a secret from the men?'

'Of course we do. Can you imagine if they knew we were off blowing a small fortune on massages and cocktails and hitting up clubs way too young for us? No way in hell.' She replaced her sunnies and looked at me. 'It's our one weekend to let loose, where no-one knows us. What happens in Melbourne stays in Melbourne. We've made a pact.'

I sucked in my lips and looked ahead, nodding as I digested the fact my mother had an entire side to her I had never gotten to know.

'Why are you bringing me?'

She grabbed my hand. 'I've been waiting years until I could bring you with me.'

A PLAN UNRAVELLED

I squeezed her hand and quietly chuckled. 'What am I in for...'

Sue, Louisa, Jackie and Martina had arrived an hour earlier. They usually took one car on their girls' trip, but didn't have the room for me to join. I asked Mum why she hadn't asked one of her friends to travel with us, and she said she hadn't thought of it, but I suspected she wanted me to herself.

The four of them have been friends for nearly forty years, so they watched me grow from baby to teen to woman. They celebrated with Mum when I made it to the big screen, and, I'm guessing, comforted her when I had my overdose. And while they were all the same age and had plenty of the same interests, they all had very different personalities.

Sue was overweight with long dark hair. She loved a flashy muu-muu and packed a kaleidoscope of colours across her round face. Her voice matched her loud exterior. Louisa was short, soft-spoken and never struck me as someone who would enjoy the city life. She got around Rockford in gumboots, trackies and a singlet covered in dirt from being in the garden all day. Her yard was always immaculate. Jackie and Martina were alike. Both were beautiful. Though cosmetically enhanced from the tips of their foreheads to their oversized chests, they were kind, fun, and didn't care about what anyone had to say about them.

When Mum and I arrived at the rental apartment, the first thing I noticed was the opened bottles of vodka, ciders and some strawberry-scented liquor on the table. Music played from speakers on the kitchen bench and there was not one yoga mat in sight.

They weren't here to relax, they were here to break free. For one weekend, they didn't have jobs to attend, errands to run or chores to do. They didn't have to answer to anyone. I wish I knew about this trip years ago. I would have joined them earlier.

Sue stood, her martini glass shaking in her hand, and ran to us. 'Oh, you've made it! Let the festivities begin!' She wrapped her arms around Mum then planted a kiss on my cheek. 'And you, Ruby. Wow, look at you. Just beautiful. It must be so nice to be back home.'

Jackie coughed, looking embarrassed.

'Nice to see you all.' I put my bag at my feet and walked to the drinks. 'Looks like we have some catching up to do!'

'Yes, girlfriend,' Martina shouted. 'Get stuck into it.'

'Are you sure that's a good idea?' Louisa chipped in, only to cop glares from Mum and the others.

'She's just fine to drink Louisa,' Mum lectured.

'I didn't mean to offend, I just…'

'That's okay.' I raised a cider. 'There's more to the story than what you've probably heard. And I'm fine.'

'Here, here,' Sue roared. 'There's always more to the story.'

A PLAN UNRAVELLED

Mum and I slipped off our shoes and joined the women on the couches. I sat back and watched as Mum morphed into a real human. One who laughed and joked and drank. She leaned her head on her friends' shoulders, sang along to the music from the radio on the bench, snorted and wiped away tears of laughter as she told the ladies about her embarrassment at the grocery store earlier in the week.

'I only needed a few things- zucchinis, carrots and cucumbers,' Mum laughed. 'I told the clerk I was looking forward to a nice evening and...' she laughed louder, 'and he winked at me!'

'Oh, you're always a crack up,' Martina hissed, after spraying a mouthful of vodka over Sue, who didn't flinch as she wiped the drops away with her hand.

'I don't get what's so funny,' Louisa asked, prompting the women to laugh harder.

'Oh, I would be having the time of my life with those items.' Sue laughed. 'All Allen has is a party frankfurt.'

'At least you're getting fed.' Jackie laughed. 'With Gordon gone off shore so much, I'm lucky if I get that frankfurt once a month.'

'Dave's home all the time, and I still don't do it once a month. I could count on one hand how many times we've had sex in the last two years.'

Louisa looked confused.

'What on earth? Are you serious?' Martina asked.

'Deadly. There's no romance in our lives anymore. But you know what? I couldn't imagine myself without him. So, romance or not, that's how it's gotta be.'

'But you'll dry up,' Sue yelled. 'You're probably already dry. Shrivelled, like a dried peach. With mould.'

They burst into laughter, Mum grabbing at her stomach. 'Oh stop it, my belly hurts.'

Sue looked at me. 'Yours would be fresh as a daisy still, wouldn't it?'

The girls laughed harder.

'No seriously,' she continued. 'What I wouldn't give to be young and beautiful, and rich and famous. You've probably got a hit list only accomplishable in my deepest fantasies.'

Mum hit her on the knee. 'Hey now, that's my daughter.'

I smiled. 'A lady never kisses and tells.'

'Oh, shush,' Sue retorted, even more boisterous from the alcohol. 'Come on now. It's gotta be better than our men. She could have anything we dream of – the firefighter, the surgeon…'

'The teacher,' Louisa surprisingly chipped in.

Jackie, Martina, Sue and Mum simultaneously turned to Louisa in shock.

'Oooo,' Jackie yelped childishly.

'What?' Louisa snapped. 'Can't I fantasise too?'

Jackie quickly continued on to squash the awkwardness with Louisa. 'The sailor,' she said. All the ladies swooned.

'The lumberjack,' Martina said, prompting more laughter.

'Lumberjack?' Jackie snorted. 'Really?'

'The gardener,' Mum said.

My smiled dropped and Mum sucked in her lips, suddenly aware of her revelation.

'Well,' Sue said, 'some of us can still fulfil our fantasies, while some of us already have.' She nodded at Mum then swallowed the rest of her drink.

The women went quiet and Mum straightened her back, avoiding eye contact with me, then excused herself to the toilet.

Jackie looked at me, searching for a smile, and I struggled to grin back.

Mum and Ron?

'So,' she changed the subject, 'these drinks are going straight to our heads.'

Mum returned a few minutes later and joined in the new topic of conversation: heels, skirts and other bargains the woman had bought, and what they wanted to find in the shopping expedition they'd planned the following day. They made a few comments about me being their personal stylist, and about how great it would be if they had the pay checks I did. I tried to pitch in, but I couldn't. I was still in shock. How could I be so blind? How could Mum hide something like that from me?

When my stomach began to turn and my toes began to tap, I knew it was time to try and shut my brain off and catch some sleep.

That night, I laid in bed, tossing and turning until the sun had risen and the birds chirped.

TWENTY-TWO

I followed the ladies in and out of stores, even picking out a few pieces for each of them and encouraging them to try on dresses they wouldn't normally wear. Mum smiled at me with worried eyes and I attempted reassurance in return.

As we walked out of one store and towards another, I noticed a small collectors' shop in a dark arcade. I remembered visiting there with Lucas when we were young. Lucas. I still had mixed feelings after he'd left the other night. I wanted to trust him, but couldn't. I wanted to apologise, but didn't feel I was in the wrong.

'I'll meet you girls back here soon. I just need to check out something.' I lowered my head to avoid the usual whispers and stares as I walked through a small crowd.

The door chimed as I entered. The locked glass cabinets against the exposed brick walls contained everything from jewellery to stamps.

'Welcome to my store.' A skinny bald man wearing glasses held together with tape stood behind a desk with a till. Boxes were spread throughout the store, filled with various items. The locked glass cabinet behind the man was full of comic books.

I should be shopping with Mum and her friends, but I couldn't turn back now. Yes, Lucas pissed me off. Yes, I feel betrayed. But he did contribute to my success. He supported every decision I made and cheered me on for years. How could I just walk past a collectors shop without at least asking about the prized comic book?

'It looks like you're moving,' I said.

'Yup. Shutting up shop,' he said. 'I'm too old to keep going. Besides, bills are piling up, rent is getting expensive, and there's not a huge demand for collector comic books anymore.'

'That's too bad.' I walked to him.

'Hey, I recognise you,' he said, shaking his finger at me. 'My wife loves your movies.'

I ran my hand over my hair and forced a smile. 'Oh, thank you.'

'I wouldn't take you for a collector of sorts.'

'Oh, I'm not, really,' I said, inching towards him. 'I know someone who is though. And he's obsessed with Action Comics.'

'Oh really? We have quite an extensive range.'

'As does he,' I said. 'He's only missing one of them, and I'm guessing it's almost impossible to get.'

'Which one?' he asked.

I thought back to mine and Lucas' conversation. 'Number seven.'

'Ahh, Action Comics number seven. Only the second time Superman appeared on the cover.' He looked me up and down. 'Got my hands on a copy about three months ago.'

'Amazing!' I smiled thinking about how thrilled Lucas would be to see his prized collection complete.

'But-' he continued. 'It's rare. Very rare.'

I nodded. 'So I've heard.'

'Which means it's very expensive,' he emphasised every word.

'I would have expected as much.' I crossed my hands, thinking about Michelle's stern warning. I didn't have a lot of money left. I couldn't be careless. 'Thank you, anyway.' I backed away and put my hand on the door, stopping to stare at the ruby on my finger. I didn't notice when I left it at Jack's. I'm sure I wouldn't miss it if it was gone for good. It didn't mean as much to me as that comic meant to Lucas.

I spun around. 'Would you consider a trade?'

'Look Anna...'

'My name is Ruby. My real name is Ruby Johns,' I said.

'Look Anna, Ruby, whoever you are. My wife is a fan, but I couldn't trade a picture or autograph for that comic.'

'How about a rare vintage ring?'

He raised an eyebrow.

'I will give you half the asking price of the magazine, plus the ring. I bought it after I moved to

New York to remind myself of who I was and where I came from. It should be enough to cover your bills and take your wife on a holiday. Or you can give it to her. And it would certainly be worth more than that comic.'

He rubbed his chin.

I twisted it off my finger and placed it in his hand. He examined it for a few moments. 'Why, if it means so much to you, would you part with it for a friend?'

'He supported my dreams when I was younger, so it's the least I could do,' I said. 'That, and I don't need a ring to remind me of who I really am. I just needed a trip back home.'

He cleared his throat, stuck the ring in his pocket and stuck out his hand. 'Okay. You have yourself a deal.'

A PLAN UNRAVELLED

TWENTY-THREE

The day rolled into an evening of more drinks and more jokes. Dressed in our new clothes and heels, we grabbed a taxi to Southbank, where we weaved between pubs, dance clubs and the casino, then settled at a blackjack table, with Sue the only winner to emerge. And the entire room knew of it. She threw her arms in the air with every win, did little dances and spins on her seat at each collection and rested her money in her ample cleavage until it began to spill over. The rest of us, defeated by the casino, the cocktails and the morning light, finally managed to convince Sue to take her winnings and shout us a cab back to the apartment, where everyone went to bed with their make-up faded and their new clothes on.

After a slow-start the next morning, we packed up, said our goodbyes and grabbed a couple coffees for the trip home. The music in the car was subdued, and Mum's wrinkles looked a little thicker and her eyes a little smaller.

As we stopped at a traffic light, I took a sip of my coffee then looked to Mum. 'Thank you for inviting me.'

'Thank you for coming, Ruby.'

'I really had a good time. It was nice to see you in that environment.'

She laughed. 'What environment, the city?'

'No, with your friends. Relaxed. Laughing. Happy looks good on you.'

She smirked. 'I look forward to that weekend every year.'

'Maybe you should do it more often.'

'Maybe.'

The light turned green and I took another sip.

'You know, I am human. I'm not just a mother, or a wife. I enjoy being those things but I don't think it defines me,' she said. 'I enjoy a good time. I like to let my hair down. I can have fun.'

I nodded.

'And I make mistakes. Just like everyone else.'

I looked at my coffee lid.

'We all make mistakes, Ruby. No one is perfect.'

'I know.'

'The important thing is that you own up to it, learn from it, and move on.'

I looked to her. 'Have you owned up to yours?'

She raised her shoulders and inhaled. 'I have.'

I swallowed the lump in my throat. 'Does Dad know?'

'Of course. I made my mistake first,' she stared ahead.

'When?' I asked.

A PLAN UNRAVELLED

'After you were born.'

'When did it stop?'

'Shortly after.'

'It did stop, right Mum? I asked, suddenly worried about Ron's recent return to Rockford.

'Yes, it stopped. I hurt your dad once, and I will never hurt him again.'

I sighed. 'I wish he had the same mentality as you.'

Mum paused. 'You know how competitive he is. If you do something, he'll make you pay. He doesn't get even. He wins. That's why he's such a good lawyer.'

I took another sip of coffee. 'Well, you shouldn't still be paying for the mistakes you made years ago.'

She exhaled slowly. 'What choice do I have?'

'You can start fresh, Mum.'

'I fear I'm too old for that,' she said. 'You, on the other hand, aren't.'

I looked at my buzzing phone. Michelle. She had called three times over the weekend and I hadn't answered once. I turned the phone off and tucked it into my handbag at me feet. I looked into the side door mirror, at the city behind me, then looked out the windscreen to the road ahead.

TWENTY-FOUR

I tossed my bags on my bed, peered out my bedroom window to see Jack's ute in his driveway, and ran next door to see him. I stood on his doorstep under the faint moonlight, with a soft breeze tickling my bare neck. When he didn't answer my knocks, I hurried to The Night Owl.

I wanted to wrap my arms around him, kiss his lips and tell him, for once in my life, I couldn't wait to get back to Rockford. And I hoped that maybe, with that news, the rest of his walls would come down and I'd finally be welcomed in.

I opened the doors to the pub, the bells chiming above my head, and spotted Jack at the end of the bar, his face lost in thought as usual, with two empty glasses beside him.

Sensing the tension, I decided against playfully throwing my hands over his eyes and kissing his cheek. Instead, I tucked my handbag against my chest and plonked myself in the empty chair next to him. I spotted Jimmy picking up glasses from a group of drunk men at a corner table.

A PLAN UNRAVELLED

Jack looked from the wall to me with his red eyes, before shifting back to oblivion.

'Hey,' I said.

Nothing.

'Are you okay?'

He looked the worse I had seen him.

'I'm fine.' He sounded drunk.

I crossed my legs and leaned in. 'You don't seem fine. You've had a few extra drinks tonight, haven't you?'

He lifted the glass to his lips, rested it there, then took a small sip.

'What's going on, Jack?'

He grabbed an entertainment magazine from the end of the bar and passed it to me.

I knew before I got to the page that there was something condemning inside. Something the paparazzi would have dug up on me to sell more magazines. Or something fabricated. Either way, I knew, it wasn't good. I slowly flipped through until I saw 'Anna Johns' in bold print, with photos of Jack and I spread across the glossy pages.

'Anna Johns in hiding in Australia,' I read quietly. 'Troubled actress Anna Johns has been spotted taking refuge in her hometown, Rockford. The actress, who nearly died of a drug overdose almost three months ago, has been defying doctors' orders. She's been spotted drinking, gambling and seeking solace in the arms of'—I slowed—'ex-con Jack Williams.' There were pictures of Jack and I in his car, kissing in his living room, talking outside, holding hands. They were zoomed in and blurry, taken assumingly by an amateur, but they couldn't be denied.

My heart sank. I'd thought that after two months, the editors of such tabloids had forgiven Anna or forgotten about the scandal. Not only had they pounced on photos of me, they had to drag Jack through the mud too. I dropped the magazine to my lap and looked to Jack, who stared into his glass.

'I'm so sorry,' I said. 'I don't know who took these photos. And these magazines are horrible at making stuff up. I've been dealing with it for years.'

'Well, it's all true. So someone's been following us and digging shit up on me. Now everyone knows. Now you know.' He spun the scotch in a circle, his eyes unwavering from his glass. 'Now you can walk away.'

My mind swirled with questions. Who took the photos? Why had Jack been withholding information about his past? What happened? But my mouth couldn't move and my eyes couldn't blink.

'You were going to leave in a couple weeks anyway, right? May as well get out now and leave this piece of shit ex-con in your past.'

'Jack...'

'Is this what you wanted? Any publicity is good publicity, right? Did you plan this?' He slurred his words and swayed. 'Because this isn't something I wanted everyone to know. I, unlike you, don't want my name and picture in magazines. I don't want everyone knowing who I am or what I did. I came here to get away from it. Not to have it plastered in magazines.'

'We all do things we aren't proud of, and I came here to run away from my past too,' I sighed. 'And I found you.'

'What's that meant to mean?'

'It means I found a future, Jack. If you want one. You just need to open up, stop hiding things from me. I know you're a good person. I know that whatever happened can't be that bad, can it?'

I didn't know, but I wanted to believe it. I wanted to believe he was a good person. I wanted to believe he, like me, was misunderstood.

He finished his drink and stood, turned his back and slowly staggered towards the door, bracing on a chair to steady himself before continuing.

I followed. Why wouldn't he just open up to me? Why had I been so vulnerable? 'I've been honest with you from the beginning. Which, apparently, is more than you can say for yourself, Jack Williams. What's your story?'

He stopped, shook his head, then continued towards the door. The drunk men's laughter echoed from the corner of the pub. One elderly man, his face brown and weathered, his tan skin clinging to his tiny bones, stood in the middle, spilling his drink. Grey greasy strands swept across a bald patch on his head and when he opened his mouth, black rot showed on his crooked teeth. He was shouting something to his friends, but I couldn't understand through the slur and spit. One of the men shook his head in embarrassment. Then the drunk called out to us, and Jack and I both stopped in our tracks.

'Well, well, well,' he spat, swaying as he walked towards us, despite a mate from his group trying to call him back. He pointed his finger towards me and poked the air. 'Rockford's claim to fame. Ruby, I mean, Anna Johns. Anna. Johns.' He laughed and coughed, then caught his breath. 'Anna Johns is sleeping with an ex-con.'

The other men laughed and rolled their eyes. 'Oh, boy,' one muttered.

'It says so in the magazines,' the old man continued.

Jack shifted his shoulders, almost sobering up at the man's approach. I walked a few steps towards the drunken man. His glossy eyes struggled to focus on me and he grabbed a table to steady his stagger.

'You're as crazy as the rest of your family.'

I looked over to the kitchen to see Jimmy standing next to Kate. Their eyes were focused on our group, waiting in worry to see what would happen next.

'Okay, that's enough,' one man in the crowd yelled. 'Leave the girl alone.'

'Nah, I'm not being nasty. I'm joking. JOKING!' He let out a howl and yelled at the group. 'This here girl is a really preeeetty thang. I loved her movies.' He turned to me. 'Loved your movies.'

Jack drew closer to me, using a table to keep from falling. Despite his anger, he grabbed my hand. 'Let's go,' he whispered.

'It doesn't surprise me that you're with him.'

'Let's go.' Jack tugged at my hand.

I let go and stepped towards the drunk, intrigued.

'Alright, that's enough,' one of the men repeated.

'I think you've had enough,' Jimmy shouted.

'I'm just playin.' The drunk nodded at me. 'Sorry, darling. On your way.'

Jack stared at him, then pulled me towards the door.

'Diddddn't you try to neck yourself not too loooong ago?' The drunk yelled as we opened the door.

My heart sank. My body felt hot.

'Couldn't get the job done,' he continued. 'Trust this guy will do it for you.'

Jack turned around with clenched fists. The world seemed to stop. Everyone froze, except that drunk. For a moment, the world was his, that bar was his platform, and his drunken words, like weapons, were the catalysts to unleash the next global war.

With a fury I'd never seen, Jack leapt from behind me onto the old man. The force threw the tables and chairs across the floor. The screeches and snaps of broken furniture, the chaotic roar of the drunken mob, the background music and the old man's pleas for help echoed in my ears as I watched the battle.

Jimmy looked frantic as I stood motionless, watching Jack deliver blows to the drunk, whose frail body had no hope against Jack's muscular frame, rage and adrenaline. Jack's elbow rose and fell, his ironclad fists pounding the old man's jaw as the mob struggled to pull him off. Blood splattered like red paint as the old man's leather skin cracked open and widened with each blow. For a moment, Jack released his fists and tightened his grip on the man's t-shirt, ripping it in two and revealing his bony chest.

I heard screaming, but didn't realise it was from me until Jimmy pulled at my waist, dragging me away from the war zone. 'It's okay, Ruby. You're okay.'

Kate yelled that she was going to call the police, but the men dissuaded her.

When Jack went back to finish his tirade, two of the men wrapped their arms around his neck and waist and pulled him off the broken, bloodied victim.

One of them held Jack's arms back while another threw punches to his stomach. With each hit, Jack's body leaned forward and spit flew from his mouth. He tried to stand up straight, but every punch crippled him back to a bent, groaning mess. His eyes were wide and cold, set on the old man who, with the help of his friends, had wiggled his way to a sitting position. The same blank look Jack always had at the end of the bar was again across his blood-stained face, and I wondered where his mind was.

'Please stop, please!' shouted Kate, holding her mobile up in the air as a threat against the angry crowd.

Her pleas were answered and they let Jack go. He grabbed his waist, spat on the ground then straightened his back. His cheeks caved in and out with each ragged breath. His veins popped through his tattoos, his bare chest rising and falling under the bloodied pieces of material hanging off his shoulders.

The old man groaned. His face was trembling, his nose twisted and gushing, a black ring had already formed at the top of his left eye, and his rotten teeth were covered in red.

'Bloody killer.' He wiped his broken lip, smearing blood on his tiny, wrinkled wrists.

'Get out!' Kate shouted at Jack, pointing at the door. 'Get out, get out!'

Jack threw the front door open and disappeared into the darkness. I wanted to chase him, but my legs wouldn't move. I felt tears fall down my cheeks, but my face was still.

'You alright?' one man asked.

I nodded and looked to Jimmy, who was clearly worried about me. 'I can take you home,' he said.

'No, no. I'll be fine.' I looked to the door.

'Don't go after him,' Jimmy warned.

'I'll be okay, Jimmy. It's okay.'

I ran past the men and desperately yelled at Jack's hunched silhouette in the distance, but he didn't stop. As I got closer, I saw the blood dripping down his cheek and that his arm was wrapped around his hunched waist. I grabbed his shoulder and he spun, a mixture of terror and vulnerability in his puffy eyes.

'I don't want to talk about it.' He was defeated.

I nodded and grabbed his hand. 'Okay.' I whispered.

We walked back in silence, my hand resting in his, our heads only moving to see the passing cars or the blowing trees. I had just uncovered so many horrible truths about Jack in such a short time, but I wasn't ready to let go of him yet. I wasn't ready to believe he was anything more than the person I had come to know.

The kettle boiled as I sat at the table and Jack showered. I made a cup of tea and continued to wait. The only noise in the house was the sound of the flowing water and my foot tapping on the floor. Steam poured out from under the bathroom door. I sipped slowly, hoping to pass the time. I thought about the anger I saw in Jack during the fight, the terror I saw in Jimmy and about the drunk old man who started it all. He said Jack was dangerous, that he had spent time in prison, that he had a dark past. I wondered how dark it could possibly be.

The water stopped and the shower door creaked open. I stared at the bottom of my empty tea cup, wishing there was more. I washed the cup, sat it next to the clean scotch glass on the dish rack and waited for Jack to emerge. After a minute or so, I decided to check on him.

I peeked around the door and used my index finger to push it open slightly. Jack stood staring at his beaten reflection in the circle he'd made on the steamed-up mirror.

'Are you okay?'

'Yeah.' He said quietly.

I walked behind him and gestured for him to stand up straight.

He stared at me with vulnerability and shame.

'Do you have any bandages?' I gently ran my finger over his stomach, avoiding the bruises and grazes he got from the force of the punches.

He opened his mirror and I moved his mouthwash and shaver and grabbed a packet of bandages. I led him to his living room couch so he could sit comfortably. I knelt down in front of him and ran a cold cloth over his stomach to wipe up any excess blood. I carefully placed the bandages over his grazes, then gently touched his hard stomach. I slid my hands slowly up his chest until I held his face and his gaze.

'Jack—'

'Let's not do this tonight.'

'Do what?' I rested my forehead on his chin.

'I don't feel like talking tonight.'

'You don't feel like talking any night,' I whispered. My body relaxed at the touch of his fingers running through my hair and his mouth pressed against my cheek.

I think he was waiting for me to hurl questions at him, but he'd been through enough for one day, so instead I put my head on his chest, careful not to lean against his bruises, and listened to his heart thump.

He needed to know that he had an ally, that the entire world wasn't against him, that I wasn't scared of him. That we could wipe our slate clean and start over, together.

'Jack,' I whispered.

'Yeah?'

'I want you to trust me. You can talk to me.'

He didn't say anything.

'Jack,' I swallowed, then looked to him. 'I love you.'

I waited for him to say something, but he didn't. He didn't move.

I sat up and put my hand on his cheek. 'I love you,' I repeated, as if he hadn't heard me the first time.

'You don't know me.'

'Jack...' I searched for words, but nothing came. I wanted him to say it back. I wanted something, anything.

'You need to leave, Ruby.'

I squinted my eyes and pulled my hand back. My stomach felt like it had copped the same punches as Jack had. 'What?'

'You should leave.' He took a deep breath and shuffled his body away from mine. 'You need to leave.'

'Why?'

'This is too much.' He rested his head in his hand, in obvious agony. 'I thought we were having fun.'

'You can't tell me you don't feel something, anything. Jack?'

He looked at me with pity, as if I were a child and he had just taken away my favourite toy. 'Ruby, I told you I didn't want anything serious.' He paused. 'I didn't ever want to hurt you.'

'Then don't,' I shot with a quiver.

His head still buried in his hand, he turned to me with watery eyes. 'You should listen to everyone else... I'm not the right person for you. I don't drive sports cars, wear nice clothes or travel to luxurious places. I work in the mines.' He lifted his chin. 'You're on the big screens. You like city lights and fame and rubbing shoulders with famous people. That's not me. And I can't give you a life even remotely like what you're used to.'

'I don't care about that.'

'I've been to prison.'

'So tell me what you did. Break and enter? Trespassing? What Jack?'

His hands fell to his lap and he looked past me, his face drawn. 'It's more complicated than that, Ruby.'

I stared at him for lingering minutes, until I couldn't make him out through the build-up of my tears. My heart raced and a lump gathered in my throat. 'Okay,' I caved. Salty tears dropped onto my lips. 'Okay, Jack. But one day you will wake up lonely and realise there was a woman who loved you, despite it all. And one day you will realise that you loved her too. And you threw it away.'

He looked at me and into my shattered soul. He parted his lips, then drew back, resting back against the couch. His eye flickered and his voice cracked. 'Just go, Ruby.'

I stood, hopeful that he would grab my hand or apologise, but he didn't.

I left, feeling as if it was I who had been beaten in that pub, that my heart was bruised and my pride shot. Crushed, conquered and simply exhausted from one hell of a battle.

TWENTY-FIVE

I called Michelle. Not because she had become agonisingly persistent, but because I needed an excuse to take my mind off Jack. It had been a week since I saw him last and I had run myself sick, literally vomiting, into the perfectly pruned rose bushes Ron had taken pride in manicuring next door. I tried to eat, but couldn't stomach the food. I couldn't sleep, but my eyes struggled to stay open. When I did manage to sleep, I dreamt about Jack.

I wondered how he coped at work while bruised and battered. I wondered if he returned to The Night Owl to drown his thoughts with scotch. I wondered if he thought about me or if he had regretted telling me to leave. And mostly, I wondered how bad his convictions were – that he felt compelled to hide them from me. I wondered if, maybe, everyone else was right about him.

Michelle's reaction to the article was just as I had expected. She asked me who took the photos and I told her I had no idea. She scorned me for not telling her about Jack so she could be prepared for the buckets of questions hurled at her by nosey journalists.

She told me it would be best to not ask Jack any follow-up questions, to stay away from him, to hit the gym then keep inside for the last couple of weeks.

'You need to focus on eating healthily and getting fit. Those pictures are not flattering, and it won't help with these auditions I've scored you.'

'Auditions? For who?'

'Well, the guys I told you about in the emails. The directors aren't well-known, but—'

'You're kidding me.'

'Anna—'

'Ruby.'

'You're still Anna to me,' she snapped. 'You can't be picky.'

Again she was on the move, her heels clunking, and horns honking in the background. I pressed one ear shut to hear her better, but it didn't help.

'Need I remind you what happened on set, during filming? It threw the entire production into chaos. They had to recast. They had to re-shoot. It was every producer's worst nightmare. And you did that Anna. YOU. So forgive me if I can't convince the Steven Spielberg's and Woody Allen's of this world to consider you for roles.'

I said nothing. Even if she had found better offers, I wasn't so sure I'd accept. She hadn't asked me what I wanted. She hadn't asked me if I wanted to return to my box of an apartment in the middle of the bustling city, where everyone squished like sardines in the subway or braved the road rage brought on by traffic-jams and constant road-works. She didn't ask me if I wanted to return to a life where everything I ate was planned out. Where places I went or what I saw had to be approved. Where every minute of my day was scheduled. Where the only friends I had were ones I worked with, temporarily, and the only men who approached me knew me only as Anna. They didn't know Ruby existed.

'I've got your flight scheduled. I'll send you the itinerary. I've also filled in your calendar for your returning week, so you can check that online. You've got a day of rest to get over the jet lag, then personal training sessions, a hair appointment, facial and a couple of interviews, which we'll go through beforehand. Then I scheduled—'

'Enough.'

'What?' Her panting stopped.

I took a deep breath. 'Enough.'

'Enough what?'

I paused. 'It's a lot to take in.'

'Of course it is, you've had a big break away. The biggest break you've ever taken. It's going to be a bit overwhelming getting back to work, but trust me, you'll feel like you never left.'

I scratched my eyebrow. 'That's what I'm afraid of.'

♥

Sam came over with wine, but the thought of downing a bottle repulsed me. We began planning her wedding, to keep from talking about Jack.

Jimmy never asked about him, but he kept his bedroom door open more than usual as an invitation to call in when I wanted to chat. I'd go to Jimmy's room, sit on the floor and we'd laugh about stupid things we did when we were younger – like the time he got stuck in the dryer while playing hide and seek, or the time I made him sit with me and my girlfriends, stuck in the middle of us, while we all took turns doing his hair and painting his nails. One of my girlfriends said something to us that day that I'd forgotten about, but stuck in Jimmy's mind like a footprint in wet cement.

'Remember when Eloise came in the house?' Jimmy asked. 'She said she had caught Mum and Dad kissing outside?'

I laughed and shook my head no. 'Why do you remember those miniscule details?'

'Because Mum wasn't home. She was on her yoga retreat.' Jimmy picked up his guitar and played a few notes. 'How was the yoga retreat anyway?'

I looked to him, sensing he knew the truth.

'I know,' Jimmy said quietly. 'I know everything.' He laid back on his bed and started strumming a tune.

'What is that?' I rested my head against his bed and let my ears soak up the music.

'I don't know, made it up.'

'It's good. You're good.'

'Thanks,' he said between chords.

'Jimmy?'

'Yeah?'

'Are you happy?'

'Sure.'

'Like, really happy?'

'Well, I'm not bringing out the sparklers and party bags. But I'm content.'

'You should leave. Do something that makes you really happy. Travel. Play music.'

He kept strumming. 'Are you happy?'

I laid on the floor and looked at the ceiling. 'I think I was at my happiest only a couple weeks ago.'

'And now?'

'Now I'm wishing it was only a couple weeks ago.'

TWENTY-SIX

'Hey you.' I held out a brown paper bag wrapped with a white lace bow.

Lucas scratched his head as he held open the door.

'I know I am probably the last person you expected to see on your door with a gift in hand, but I wanted to give you a peace offering.'

He waved me in. 'Peace offering?'

'I was a bit hard on you the other night.' I walked to the couch and placed the bag on the coffee table, next to a glass of wine and a cheese platter. Lucas filled another glass of red in the kitchen and returned with it in hand.

He sat next to me. 'Thank you.' I took the glass. 'I shouldn't have been so upset with you about the job thing. If you want to work with Dad, I should support you. You've supported me. I just wish you'd been upfront with me.'

'I wouldn't have considered it, but once I realised that you had no interest in reuniting a romance, I thought, Why not?'

I licked my lips.

'Maybe I should have said something.' He sighed. 'I'm sorry, but in no way would I ever use you.' He put his hand on my knee. 'You know that, don't you?'

I looked into his eyes, then at the bag on the table. 'Open it.'

He slowly untied the bow and peeled open the bag, his mouth dropping as he eased the comic out. 'Shit.'

I smiled.

'Ruby, How did you get this?'

'Just lucky, I guess.'

'This would have cost a mint. I can't accept this.'

'Please,' I said. 'I owe you for everything you did for me in high school. All the encouragement, the sacrifices. And then I made you feel terrible for going for what you wanted.'

He smiled.

'Just keep it, please. You deserve it.'

He raised the comic book in the air like a trophy and shouted like he had won a 100-metre dash. 'I can't believe this!' He lowered it to his lap and pulled me in for a hug. 'This is the nicest thing anyone has ever done for me.'

His cheek was against mine, and his hand rested on the bare skin of the small of my back, under my white cotton t-shirt. I soaked up the touch of a man's hand against my skin, and for a moment, imagined it was Jack. Ten days had passed since I had seen him last and each day was one day closer to boarding the plane back to my old life in America.

Lucas slowly moved his head until the cold tip of his nose brushed against my nose and I could feel his heavy breath on my lips. And then he kissed me.

I instantly remembered the way he tilted his head, the way his mouth pressed hard against mine, the way he tasted. But this time, there was no spark. No goose bumps. Nothing that resembled the feelings I had for Jack. I pulled back slowly.

'Sorry.' He lowered his head. 'I've done it again. Just thrown myself out there.'

I scratched my ear. 'Don't be sorry.'

He grabbed his wine, took a swig and leaned back against the couch, his eyes resting on the comic.

I sat in silence, then picked up the comic book and handed it to him. 'Keep this as a reminder of how special you are to me.'

He smiled. 'I still can't believe you got me this. Amazing. You're one in a million.'

'As are you.'

He walked to his locked cabinet, looked inside, then closed it again. 'I can't just stick this in here. It's gotta be framed.'

'I can get you a frame.'

'Nah, I should have spares in the study.'

I followed him down the hall, my glass in hand, and stood behind him as he shuffled through the boxes in his closet looking for a photo frame large enough to fit his new prized magazine. He reached to a box on the top shelf, sending papers and pictures plummeting to the floor.

'Oh.' I put my wine on his desk and got on my knees to help pick them up. 'Hopefully you don't need this in any particular order.'

He grabbed them from my hand and shoved them back on the shelf. 'No, just old paperwork I should probably archive.'

I went to grab my wine as he returned to his search, but my eyes fell on a picture of me, which peeked out of some paperwork on his desk. I moved the papers aside to see four images of Jack and I. The same ones that were in the magazine. My heart thumped and toes tapped.

I picked up the papers – official police documents and old newspaper articles, which had been printed off the computer.

The police document was dated the year 2000, and had a photo of Jack and a list of charges.

The first article had appeared in the Brisbane Times:

"Three Dead, One Charged"

Three people are dead and one person is fighting for their life in hospital after an alleged burglary went wrong on the weekend. Police allege three youths were involved in a break and enter shortly after midnight on Saturday. It is believed the sole occupant of the house, aged in his eighties, shot all three offenders, killings two and injuring another. The injured intruder was taken to hospital and is expected to be charged at a later date. Police said the occupant of the house was found dead in his house with a self-inflicted injury.

The second article was dated only a few weeks later.

Brisbane resident Jack Michael Williams, 19, has pleaded guilty at the Brisbane Magistrates Court for break and enter and attempted burglary. He was sentenced to five years in prison and will be eligible for parole in three years. Judge Marla Vickers said the case was a 'break and enter gone horribly wrong.'

Lucas was watching me, a frame dangling in his hand. A look spread across his face and the colour disappeared from his face.

Tears welled. My palms sweated. I struggled to speak as I raised the paperwork. 'What is this?'

Silence.

'What is this, Lucas?'

'Let me explain.'

'Please do.'

'Your dad asked me to—'

'My dad?' My voice shook. 'Asked you what? To spy on me?'

'In a sort.' He stepped closer and I backed up.

A PLAN UNRAVELLED

'You spied on me? You sold the story? You sold me out? You told me I could trust you.'

'We wanted to protect you.'

'Protect me?' I shrieked.

He gathered his breath and placed the frame on the desk next to me. 'I'm telling you the truth, Ruby. Your dad had concerns about Jack. When I expressed interest in the job, he asked for a favour and when he said it was to protect you, I couldn't refuse.'

I shook my head in disbelief.

'He knew I had connections in the police force.'

'And so does he.'

'He didn't want to have that paperwork on his hands, in case you found it. He said he was going to speak to you about it, but you wouldn't listen to him.

'He said you only listened to Michelle. I thought he was going to send her the information. I didn't know he had photos, and I didn't know he was going to sell the story to the tabloids.'

I shook my head again. 'If he took the photos, how come you have them?'

'He dropped them off yesterday... when he offered me a job.'

'Well,' I sputtered. 'Congratulations. You lost a friend and gained your dream job. Bravo.'

We stared at each other, defeat heavy in our eyes, knowing we had both lost something special. There was no coming back from this.

TWENTY-SEVEN

'You're packed?' Jimmy stood at my doorway. 'You still have three days left.'

I zipped my suitcase, sat it on the floor and patted the bed beside me. I'd just finished telling Dad that if he kept betraying everyone he loved, he would have no-one left. He'd replied it was for my own good and apologised, but I'd refused to forgive him. I didn't want his betrayal to take a toll on my life, like it had on my mother's. I should have expected nothing less.

Jimmy sat, his shoulder against mine, and stared out the window. Ron popped in and out of eyesight, earphones around his dark face and a whipper snipper in hand.

'Rockford hasn't convinced you to stay?' He let out a dry laugh tainted with sadness.

'It's chewed me up and spat me out, Jimmy.'

'New York did too, remember?'

I rested my head on his shoulder. 'I'm giving it another shot. Maybe you should come with me.'

'Nah, not my thing.'

'You could busk?' I laughed, still knowing the answer.

'I could busk here too.'

I smirked at his stoned face. 'Why don't you?'

'What? Busk?'

'Well, if you'd rather wash dishes your whole life that's okay too… but wouldn't it be more fun to make a few extra dollars on the side, doing something you actually enjoy? You said it yourself.'

'No-one would give me money to hear me play a guitar.'

'I would.'

'You're my sister.'

'Think about it. You need to spread your wings. Do something you want to do.'

'Likewise,' he said. 'Keywords sis, "something you want to do".'

'I can't believe Lucas and your dad! Scandalous.' Sam scanned the dress section of a wedding magazine, flipping past each page as if it burned her hand to touch. She held a latte in her other hand but had barely taken a sip since the waitress handed it to her fifteen minutes prior. 'I didn't see that coming. Just, you know, because they are two very different people.'

'Apparently not.' I watched the line of cars pass the café. It was unusual for so many to drive by at once.

Sam stopped on a page with a white princess-style dress with a sequined bustier and layers of tulle.

'You can't tell me you like that one!'

She laughed. 'No. But it has crossed my mind to walk down the aisle in a big puffy dress, a lot of bling and a face full of make-up. Ha. How funny would Harry's face be? He'd be like, "Who even are you?" and I'd be like "Do you ever really know the person who love? Do ya? Stuck with me now!"'

I turned to her with raised eyebrows. 'Here, here.'

'Oh, come on. I don't think Lucas or your dad were trying to hurt you. I think they genuinely care about you and you've been through a lot lately, they just wanted to protect you. They just did it in the wrong way. It blew up in everyone's face.' She took a sip of her latte and shrugged at the taste. 'They gave me a cold latte!' She looked over her shoulder, hoping to get the waitress's attention.

'It was hot when they gave it to you.'

She slid the latte aside. 'I'm after more of a bohemian dress to go with my beach wedding anyway.'

'Beach wedding? That sounds more your style.'

'Yup. You get to wear a toga style bridesmaid dress.'

I leaned across the table. 'Me? Bridesmaid dress?'

'Oh right,' she squealed. 'I haven't asked you, have I?'

I shook my head no and grinned in anticipation.

Sam cleared her throat and closed her magazine. 'Ruby Johns. I have known you a long time…'

We both giggled like high school students as she made her speech.

'You have been there for me through my good times, and the dark times. When we lost touch, I always felt like a part of me was missing. And when you returned, only a few short months ago, I felt whole again.'

I rolled my eyes.

'Now. I know you are leaving me again, but this time, I won't let the distance divide us.'

I erupted into laughter.

'Will you do me the honour of being my maid of honour?'

'Of course, Sam.'

'Yay!' She reached across the table and wrapped her arms around me. 'That means you have to come back next year to be part of it all. You will have to schedule whatever blockbuster movie you are working on around the wedding of the year, okay? And I am expecting a kick-ass hen's day, with monkeys and a bubble machine and a hot, triplet stripper act – dressed as firemen. No, as police. No, as three-fifths of N'Sync. Actually, just give me three Justin Timberlands.'

'Timberlake?'

'You say potato, I say potata.'

'I'll give you a party that will go down in the history books.' I laughed. 'Maybe jelly-wrestling, pie-eating, and a Mike Brady look-alike draped in only whipped cream.'

Sam's eyes widened. 'You remember my high school crush! I never missed an episode of the Brady Bunch.'

'I remember how no-one was allowed to call you while you were watching the re-runs.' I smiled.

She raised her hand to her heart and shook her head in pride. 'You just get me. Now,' she snapped, 'I have to get going. Harry wants to look for a cool combi van or something to hire for the wedding. I told him only hippy musicians drive those things, but he's set on it.'

'Yeah?' My mind turned to Jimmy. 'Maybe I'll come with you.'

I leant on the horn several times as I drove the rusty burnt orange combi van down the driveway. Mum and Jimmy came running out.

'What is this bomb?'

I patted the front of it and tossed Jimmy the keys. 'It's your new home, brother.'

A questioning grin crept up his cheek, as he gazed over the van. 'What?'

'It's your new home,' I repeated. Michelle would no doubt lecture me for spending most of the money left in my account, but I'd left enough to ensure I could live modestly in New York for a month of two.

'Ruby Johns. What are you talking about?' Mum asked with the same assertiveness she used when I was younger. 'Jimmy can't live in that.'

'Why not? Sure he can.' I winked at Jimmy. 'There's a bed for you, room for an esky, and space for your guitar.'

He opened the sliding door and ducked his head inside. Mum crossed her arms around her chest and stood beside me as Jimmy disappeared inside.

'He doesn't know how to take care of himself,' she whispered loudly. 'How do you think he'll go travelling around Australia without a clue on how the world works? He has to pay for petrol, for services, for food, for—'

'Mum, he's a grown man, he needs to learn.'

Jimmy emerged and sauntered to us, his fingers shaking at his sides. 'It's cool. I just, I dunno—'

'What's not to know?' I asked. 'Life's too short to spend it living holed up in your parents' house.'

Mum threw me a look.

'Just give it a shot. Take a chance.'

He nodded.

The sun ducked behind a cloud and a cold chill crept over me. Our conversation was interrupted by the sound of another engine purring in the neighbour's driveway. Ron had just pulled up and shyly lifted his hand when all three of us looked at him.

I watched Mum's chest rise and toes tap as Ron closed the car door and walked towards our fence.

'Nice van,' he shouted.

'It's Jimmy's.' I walked up to the fence and Jimmy followed.

Mum stayed a few metres back. 'He's going to road trip, funded by his guitar apparently.'

'I didn't know you played!' Ron looked surprised.

'I do.' Jimmy lowered his chin and dragged a small pebble across the pavement with his faded sneakers.

'Well,' Ron huffed. 'I think that's great. You have to follow your heart. If it doesn't work out, then at least you know you gave it a shot. No regrets.'

Mum lifted her head, agitated, her toe tapping quicker. Ron, perhaps noticing, lifted his fingers to his head and saluted. 'Good luck with it all, Jimmy.'

'Thanks.'

Ron turned back to the neighbour's house. I glanced between his departing figure and Mum's saddened eyes.

Jimmy turned to Mum who had wiped a single tear from the corner of her eye. 'I won't be gone for long.'

Her neck jolted from Ron to Jimmy. 'What?'

'I won't be gone for long, don't be so upset. I'll come back when I need money.' He laughed.

'You won't need money, Jimmy,' I butted in. 'You've got some stashed away. Sleep in parking lots, get a few gigs at pubs. You'll find your way. You may hit a speed bump or two, but you'll find a way. I'm sure of it.'

'I hope this thing can handle a speedbump or two,' he joked, walking to the van and bending at his knees to inspect the worn tires.

'Trust me, Jimmy.'

He held his fist forward, and I knocked his knuckles with mine. 'I trust you,' he said.

'Now, are you going to take me for a spin before you start planning the road trip?' I walked to the passenger side and opened the creaky door.

He spun the keys around his fingers and made a small hop before bouncing to the driver side. 'Okay. Okay.' He sat in the driver's seat and turned to Mum. 'You want to come? There's room for you in the back!'

She shook her head. 'I don't think so.'

TWENTY-EIGHT

I had found momentary relief from both Jack and Lucas's betrayal through packing, Sam's coffee date and the purchase of Jimmy's new van, but when I lay in bed at night, my mind raced and stomach turned. I was due to board the plane in less than twenty-four hours and was leaving with a broken heart, a frazzled head and more of my life in pieces than when I'd arrived.

I wasn't ready to close the door on Jack, yet. Everything had become clear. He'd told me not to fall in love, to protect me – the same way Lucas and my dad wanted to protect me, only they hurt me in doing so.

I cried because I was scared Jack wouldn't let me in, and I cried because I didn't know what else to do. I cried, then I slept, then I cried some more until there were no tears left. My stomach turned. Then I vomited until there was nothing left to vomit. I hugged the toilet, wiped my eyes and mouth, then looked into the mirror at a broken woman – reminiscent of the broken woman who had lain in her hospital bed only three months prior. I stared into my red eyes and wet cheeks.

I managed to squeeze in a few hours of sleep, then did my best attempt to hide the puffy bags under my eyes with concealer and blush. Mum and Dad had planned a family dinner to farewell both Jimmy and I, but I had a couple of goodbyes to say first.

I stopped at The Night Owl, where Sam was pouring pints for a group of miners.

'Hey, you. I was hoping you'd stop in before you left,' she yelled across the bar.

She met me half way through the room, where, the last time I'd stood here, Jack was copping a series of hard punches.

'You excited to go back?'

'Back to honking horns, tourists and a list of demands? Oh, so excited,' I muttered. 'I'm not sure I'm ready.'

She tilted her head and wrapped her arms around me. 'Well, you can always come back.'

'I'm gonna miss you,' I whispered in her ear. I could have told Sam I was happy for her. That I was proud she wasn't the same person I'd known before I moved to New York over a decade ago, or that she had her own successful business, or that she had found someone who made her as happy as she made him. I wanted to say thank you to her for believing in me, for listening to me, for not judging me. But I didn't. There was still time. I lifted my wrist to her to show the dangling pendant on my bracelet. She lifted hers too and grabbed my hand.

'Well, get going you. I have a feeling I'm not the only person you want to say goodbye to,' she said.

I took a deep breath, assuming she meant Lucas. 'I haven't spoken to him for days.'

'Well, he hasn't been back in the bar since that fight.' She glanced at the empty seat where Jack usually sat. 'Maybe you should check up on him.'

I looked to the seat then back at Sam. 'Maybe.'

I waited outside his door for half an hour. I drove past the mine to see his car was missing from the car park. I thought about texting, or calling, but it wasn't until I sat at the kitchen table, skimming through the paper while Mum made one last family meal, that I spotted Jumping Jack listed on the race guide and knew where I would find him.

I spotted him, in beautiful solitude, with a race book in hand, black sunnies on his unshaven face, leaning against the fence, looking lost in thought.

Butterflies leapt from the pit of my stomach, sending a flutter to my heart, then stopped in the midst of my throat. I swallowed, but couldn't shake the anxiety. 'You winning?' I took my spot beside him and leant my elbows over the fence. I could feel him glance at me then turn back to the empty track.

'Nope.' His voice was cold. He tapped the race book against his hand. 'Down on my luck.'

I looked up at him, one shut eye against the glare of the sun. I raised my hand over my eyes to shield the light. 'How have you been?'

'Fine.'

'Really?'

'Really.'

I sighed and lowered my hand. 'Jack...' I pleaded. 'Please don't shut me out.'

'Ruby...' He turned to me and rested his race book by his side. 'Don't do this.'

'What?'

'This... trying to make us something we aren't.' He leaned his elbow against the fence and raised his sunnies to the top of his head. 'I can't get into the same place as you.'

'You mean you can't love me?'

He didn't answer. The nerves wrestled in my stomach and my toes tapped.

'Don't you have a plane to catch?'

I paused. 'Tell me to stay.'

His blue eyes finally rested on mine. His face was steady and the noise of the crowd gathering around us faded to the background. For a moment, we stood in complete silence.

'I can't,' he whispered, turning back to the track.

I stared at him, hoping he'd change his mind. What was holding him back? What was scaring him? 'I know what happened to you, Jack. And if that's what you're afraid of, you shouldn't be. That was a long time ago and you served your time.'

'Did I?' he snapped back.

The horses left the barrier and the crowd erupted in cheers.

'I served a few years in jail. Is that enough?'

'Jack...' I shook my head at him in pity. 'They made bad choices, too.'

'I did it to get quick cash for my Mum after Dad left her. She wasn't coping. So I started hitting up some houses. Leo helped, but Rose had no idea.' A pale shade of white swept across his face and veins popped in his neck. He shook his head in anger.

'Jack,' I said softly, 'tell me.'

'I thought you knew.'

'Tell me your story.'

'Leo and I had done it so many times it was like second nature to us. Then one night, we asked Rose to park while we got something from a mate's. She didn't know.' He clenched his fist and looked to the sky. 'Turns out someone was home. A drunk, crazed, elderly man branding a shotgun.'

My mouth rested open and my body was still as everyone hollered in the grandstands. 'A drunk, elderly man. Like the guy from the pub?'

He looked past me. 'He got Leo, then he got me. I made it into Rose's car, and he got her.'

I wanted to hold him and tell him it was okay, but I couldn't.

'I killed them that night. I did it.'

'No, you didn't.' I tried to grab his hand, but he pulled away. 'You didn't, Jack.'

The horses flew past the finish line and screams echoed from behind us.

'I should have gotten a life sentence. I should still be locked up,' he yelled over the crowd.

I grabbed his hand, moved closer and whispered in his ear, 'Seems to me like you're serving a life sentence.'

He pulled his hand away again, raised his chin to the air and inhaled until his cheeks rounded. He dropped his sunnies back over his eyes and looked down the empty track, exhaling slowly.

'Jack.'

'Don't,' he said. 'You wanted to know. Now you know.'

'Everyone deserves a second chance.' Tears poured down my cheek. 'You aren't the only person with scars, Jack. Some of ours just aren't visible.'

I turned from him and elbowed my way through the punters. I resisted the urge to look back, because if he was looking, it would give me hope.

I didn't see one camera flash, or hear my name get called. I didn't feel like I needed to hide my swollen eyes or wet nose.

TWENTY-NINE

I ate my burger slowly, appreciating each crumb of carb that touched my tongue. I sunk my teeth into it and listened to Dad talk about working with Lucas and his upcoming weekend business meetings. I avoided eye contact and didn't speak much, the betrayal still weighing heavily on my mind.

Mum spoke about another yoga retreat she was thinking about attending with her friends, and she snapped at Dad when he laughed at her. 'What a joke. You're not a spring chicken anymore.'

'Why are you always so condescending?' she yelled back. Then, like nothing had happened, Dad asked if Mum paid the house insurance bill, and she talked about changing insurers, then went off on a tangent about also changing energy providers and what deals the neighbours were getting. For a moment, they seemed to forget they hated each other, then Mum spilled her water and Dad snapped at her again and the cycle continued.

Jimmy was slopping pieces of lettuce and tomato onto the notepad next to his plate, while jotting down travel notes. His first stop would be in Queensland. He drew asterisks by the towns he wanted to spend a few days in.

I pushed my empty plate aside and disrupted Mum from another stoush with Dad by wrapping my arms around her neck and kissing her on the cheek.

She smiled, and hugged me back.

'It's time for me to go.'

'Ruby,' Dad said.

I looked at him for the first time in days.

'I've said it before, and I will say it again. I'm sorry. I know you don't want protection, but as your father, that's what I am meant to do. That's what I want to do. I just did it horribly.'

'You're right,' I said under my breath. 'You did it horribly.'

There was a sadness in his eyes I hadn't seen since I'd first left home. I realised then that he would always see me as his little girl.

'Give me time. I'll forgive you,' I said.

'I hope so.'

'I will.'

THIRTY

Floating in clouds thousands of feet above the vicious seas, I looked out the window through tired eyes and rattled my brain with the looming schedule that would greet me in New York. Instead of getting lost in mountains of worry, I should have been appreciating the calmness of the skies.

Knots manifested in my stomach and my eyeballs stung. Tension crept into my head and I fought it by popping two painkillers. The air hostess kept asking if I was okay while forcing an approving smile. She obviously knew about my past and, when I saw her pitied look, I remembered too. I couldn't escape it. After she was out of sight, I spat the pills into my napkin and rubbed by throbbing head.

I pulled a blanket over my legs and lay back, feeling protected by my earphones and the minimal space my seat provided. I wanted to ask for a wine to ease my nerves and help me sleep, but after copping the sympathetic looks from the crew, I refrained.

I tried to shut my brain off, but I kept thinking about my awaiting shoe-box of an apartment, the meetings ahead, my physical appearance, potential interviews and fashion shoots. It seemed so overwhelming. Cameras, scripts, rules and regulations.

I closed my eyes and thought of Jack, wondering who would keep him company now that I was gone. I wondered if he thought of me. I wondered if he loved me. I wondered if he would ever forgive himself.

I must have drifted off to sleep, because I woke to the concerned air hostess prompting me to raise my seat. She smiled politely as she handed me some mints and a warm cloth for my face.

As soon as we landed, the butterflies took over, and I grabbed the sick bag hidden in the pocket beside me. As I scrambled to open it, a surge forced its way from my stomach and up my throat. I felt the stare of the well-dressed man across the aisle from me as last night's dinner made its way into the narrow hole. I wiped my chin and folded the top of the bag over, embarrassed.

'Here you are.' The air hostess stood at my side with a bottle of water and a rubbish bag. I dropped the vomit bag in and took the bottle from her.

'I just wanted to let you know I'm a huge fan,' she said, bending towards me and surely able to catch a whiff of my misery.

'Um, thank you.'

'We aren't supposed to say things like that, but I've always looked up to you. I want to be an actress.' Her refreshing innocence showed her young age.

'That's okay. I won't tell the captain,' I said. 'And thank you, but it's hard work. There's a lot of pressure. There's no privacy. And it can take its toll.'

She leaned in close. 'I work well under pressure. I want my photo across every magazine. And as for as taking its toll, try sorting out hundreds of hot meals in a shoe box, cleaning hot coffee off disgruntled passengers after a bout of turbulence and not maintaining one proper relationship because you're in three different counties in seven days. I think I could hack it.'

I smiled. 'Maybe you could.'

'I hope you feel better soon.' She stood and gave me a wink.

'Thanks.' I looked out onto the airport runway, dreading the thought of the life that awaited in New York.

THIRTY-ONE

May

Brown frozen slush lined the narrow footpaths and the roads were covered with dirt. Leaves had begun to sprout amongst bare trees and bush twigs. The chirps of the young birds, the warmth of the sun and the green tips of grass peeking their way through puddles were all signs that spring had sprung in New York.

I was pushed into a whirlpool of meetings, gym sessions and an endless stack of scripts. I struggled to keep afloat. Michelle had organised lunches and coffee dates, but before each meeting, we had a briefing where she would run through what I could say and what I shouldn't say. She insisted I stay low-key in the evenings and had late-night gym sessions in an attempt to meet strict fitness goals set out by my personal trainer.

Michelle was constantly looking over my shoulder for paparazzi or sending me warning texts when she knew where they were.

'We're going to make sure their first snap of you is when you're looking your best. A couple more weeks in the gym should do it. And we should look at a personal shopper, and maybe extensions.' She twirled her finger through my hair.

I twitched and ran my finger over the strands of hair she pulled. 'I kinda like it short.'

'Really? It's a bit of a hack job.' She scrunched her face, then swung her chair towards the back of her office and grabbed another script off a pile of messy papers.

'Here.' She handed it to me. 'This came in today.'

The Lonely Girls, written and directed by David P. Hover.

'David Hover? I've never heard of him.' I handed the script back.

'You can't be picky, Anna.' She set the script on the desk and leaned in, crossing her arms over the mess. 'I'm trying everything I can to get people to give you a chance. Everyone's worried you'll have another episode.'

'Episode?'

She twisted her hand in the air. 'Er, whatever it was. You know what I mean.'

I took a deep breath and rubbed my hand on the back of my neck.

Michelle looked at the clock. 'It's almost six. You should get to the gym. And take the script with you. Read it tonight.'

My eyes widened and I took another deep breath.

'Please, Anna,' she huffed, the script hanging loosely as she reached out to me.

'Okay. I'll read it.'

'Thank you. See you tomorrow,' she yelled as I opened the door. 'We have a meeting with the casting agent of The Wicked King at Giorgio's on fifth. Ten sharp. Don't be late.'

'Yup.' I closed the door and, like Groundhog Day, attended another gruelling personal training session. It was my sixteenth in the twelve days since I'd landed. My body ached and my dry eyes hurt. I resorted to strong coffee. By the time I was able to get to bed at night, I lay awake thinking of Jack. I wanted to call him, to ask if he missed me, to tell him I missed him. Every night I drifted off thinking of him, and he would creep his way into my dreams, and be there, in the centre of my mind when I woke. They were the best moments of my day.

After my gym session, I came home to a quiet and bare apartment and took a long hot shower. I rubbed the knots in my shoulders and dug my fingers into my achy thighs hoping to release the tension. I ran my hands over my closed eyes and left them there for a few seconds, appreciating my time alone.

It was almost nine by the time I dried off and put my pyjamas on. I looked at my mobile. I'd missed several calls from my mother and one from Sam. I hadn't spoken to them in days and thought it was a weird coincidence they both decided to phone me the same evening, but I was too exhausted to call them back. I flicked on the television and rummaged through my refrigerator for something to eat. I'd been set up with a meal plan, each container marked with a day of the week so that I stuck to the diet. I grabbed the poached pear and chicken salad I'd been instructed to eat that evening, and curled up on my white leather couch.

I cringed at the bland lettuce leaves and picked around for the dried cranberries and pear pieces. When those were gone, I set the container of dry salad on the coffee table, next to my laptop, and switched the channels. When there was nothing that sparked my interest, I picked up my laptop and waited for it to start up.

My eyes were growing heavy and I almost flicked the laptop shut to retreat to my bed, but the homepage, still stuck on Australian News, flashed up and woke me as if I'd been hit with a freezing bucket of water.

"Several Feared Dead in Coal Mining Explosion"

My gut clenched and twisted. I dialled my mother's number, but the busy signal sounded like a loud siren through the earpiece. My body shook as I tried to find the International News Network. I gripped my phone tightly and held the remote up to my thumping heart as pictures of the disaster unfolded before me.

There were fire trucks and ambulances and police holding worried people back.

I scrolled through the contacts on my mobile and pressed on Jack's name, holding my breath and clenching my fist. 'Pick up, pick up, pick up.' After several rings, it sounded: 'The person you are trying to call is not available...' I tried again, repeatedly, until I had another call come though.

'Darling?' Mum sounded frantic. 'Are you okay?'

'What's going on?'

'There's been an explosion at the mine—'

'I know that.' I shook, surprised at the fear in my voice. 'Is he okay? Is Jack okay?'

'I don't know. I don't know. Your dad is there and I can't get a hold of him. Everyone's trying to help the fire crews and police. It's a big rescue operation right now.'

'How many?' I couldn't bring myself to say the word dead.

'I don't know. I... I don't know anything.' Her stuttered voice was low and soft. 'I wish I could tell you more. I'll keep trying to find out.'

'What happened?' My voice cracked as I tried to hold back tears.

'I'm not sure. But I could hear it. I was just making dinner and heard this loud bang and the house kind of shook. I thought at first it was an earthquake, then I heard the sirens and knew right away they were headed to the mine. There's been speeding cars, helicopters and… it's just chaos, Ruby. I've never seen anything like it.'

'I need to know if Jack was there. He won't answer his phone.'

'I went next door, he's not home. I'll keep trying your dad and see if he can find anything out.'

'Call me when you know anything, okay?'

'Okay, I promise.'

I moved to the floor, tucked my arms around my knees and rocked. Helpless and fearing the worst. I looked at my mobile. I had made a dozen unanswered calls to Jack.

I tried to text him, but my hurried fingers kept falling on the wrong keys. It took me several attempts to finally work it out.

Text me please. I need to know you are safe.

I laid my phone by my side and looked at the ceiling. Knots turned in my stomach and I rushed to the kitchen, bent over the bin and hurled out every bit of poached pear and chicken I'd managed to choke down. My eyes watered, my throat burned and my stomach felt bruised.

The television flicked from images of smoke and flashing emergency lights to broadcasters who appeared lost for information. I sat for almost an hour, watching the disaster, trying to scour the images for Jack but couldn't recognise any faces amongst the ambulances and police cars, or in the crowd of rescue workers, bystanders and miners.

My fingers held my lips tightly, and my toes tapped uncontrollably, only stopping at the sound of my ringtone.

'Mum?'

'He was working, Ruby.'

A piercing numbness stung my cheeks and my body went limp. My mobile fell from my open hand and my head slumped. I let out a wild shriek that echoed through the room.

Tears soaked my chin and wet my clothes as I fumbled to pick up the phone.

'Mum?'

'Yes, honey?'

'Is he alive?'

'I don't know, I don't know.' She paused and listened to me sob and sniffle. 'Dad has the name of about a hundred miners who were on shift, and most are still unaccounted for.'

I sobbed louder and grabbed at my stabbing chest pain. 'I'm coming home. I'm coming home now.'

'I'll be waiting, Ruby.'

THIRTY-TWO

I wasn't sure what I had packed. I had grabbed an armful of clothes from my closet, shoved it in my suitcase and pressed down hard against the jumbled pile until the zip closed. I had sent Michelle a text to say I was leaving New York and told her to cancel my meetings. I then spent the entire car trip to the airport pressing ignore on her persistent calls. She sent a few angry texts, demanding that I call her back, but I deleted each one before I could read the entire message.

I got on the first available flight, stuck between a well-dressed middle-aged man and a thin, elderly woman who sensed my distress. She looked over my shoulder as I checked my phone for regular updates and patted me on the shoulder every time I let out a sniff or a sigh.

I turned on my Wi-Fi and kept pressing for regular updates, which consisted of a slowly rising death toll.

Three dead. Then six. Then eight.

The elderly woman signalled to the air hostess. 'Can you please grab the young lady a cup of tea and a warm blanket please? We need to get some colour into her face.'

I tried to flash her a grateful smile.

I finished my tea and wrapped the blanket around my neck, tucking my chin into my chest. As the passengers slept around me, unfazed by the relentless turbulence, I struggled to keep my eyes closed. I felt suffocated, as though I were being buried alive. Each passing hour was one more pile of sand dumped on my breaking chest. I wanted out. But I feared that even when I got off that flight, even in the Australian sun I would feel as if I were stuck in a New York winter – where the bitter cold would pierce my skin and the days would be dark and dreary. It was a winter I had once fallen in love with as a young child, before ever stepping foot in sub-zero temperatures. A winter I had once chased, but once I got it, made me feel trapped and alone.

The only way I'd enjoy a New York winter now was if Jack was with me.

And if I didn't have a gruelling schedule.

And if I wasn't acting.

Actually... New York didn't appeal to me at all anymore.

I knew right where I wanted to be.

THIRTY-THREE

Mum was waiting patiently at the arrival gate. I wrapped my arms around her and held her close, my nose buried into her shoulder, and she clenched her hands around my back.

Once we got in her car, she drove as fast as her foot, and conscience, would let her. Every time I glanced over her shoulder to read the speedometer, her foot pressed down harder.

'I just can't believe this is happening. Not in this day and age. Dad said there is going to be a huge legal case…'

'I'm not even thinking about the legal matters now, Mum. I'm more concerned about—'

'I know. I know.' She put her hand on mine. 'But someone's at fault for this. For this carnage.'

I stared out my passenger side window, remembering how just a few months ago I was on the same road, worried only about my sanity and future. Now I worried that the one person I wanted in my future wouldn't be alive when I returned. I worried that I would see his cold, lifeless body lying in the morgue.

A PLAN UNRAVELLED

That I wouldn't be able to feel his warm hands on me anymore, or see his piercing blue eyes.

My chest grew heavy, like a pile of bricks had been dropped on it, and my cheeks quivered. A pain rushed behind my eyes and settled in the middle of my forehead. I grabbed at the pain.

'I can't lose him, Mum, I can't.'

It was more than twenty-four hours since the explosion, but as we arrived in Rockford, it was as though the disaster had only just struck. Trees were still, streets were bare and most shops were closed as everyone wanted to help with the rescue efforts in any way they could. Cooks and bakers from local restaurants were delivering food and drinks to emergency crews, workers, volunteers and families who waited at the mine.

I raised my hands to my chin and clasped my fingers together as we got closer to the mine. There was red tape everywhere, helicopters hovering, firetrucks and ambulances. Two police officers directed us to park our car near a line of others about a kilometre from the mine.

Before Mum could turn the car off, I had unbuckled my seatbelt and was racing past a line of people who looked like they had been there for a while. Others were sitting on blankets, holding vigils with candles and cards. I spotted a priest talking to worried adults. The police, firefighters and SES were keeping everyone who wasn't part of the rescue missions behind orange tape and portable, roped-off fences. I made my way as far forward as I could, Mum close behind, trying to see past the television vans and emergency vehicles.

I frantically searched for someone who might be able to tell me something. An ear-splitting scream penetrated the crowd and everyone turned to a woman who had fallen to her knees. A man stood behind her with his hands under her arms, holding her slightly above ground. He lowered his head. Her eyes were shut and her mouth was open with despair, letting out a silent cry. The clothes she wore were wet and splattered with a days' worth of dirt.

Two police officer stood with them, one carrying a notepad loosely by his side. If they had delivered bad news to families before, you wouldn't have known it. Their shoulders were slumped and there was little expression on their pale faces. They looked emotionally-drained.

I was locked in the woman's despair. Mum wrapped her arms around me and I tucked my head under her chin, feeling a small comfort in the stroke of her hand over my head and the press of her lips on my forehead. For a moment, I felt like a helpless child.

When the police officers left the wailing woman to grieve, Mum squeezed my hand then let go as she rushed to quiz the police officer with the notepad. She pointed and he looked at me, then ran his finger over his notepad, stopping half way through the page. I

A PLAN UNRAVELLED

lifted my shoulders, took a deep breath and held strong, preparing for the crippling news.

Mum nodded repeatedly at the police officer, then rushed to me. 'Get in the car. Jack was taken to hospital about three hours ago.'

I gasped and let my shoulders fall. I could feel my heart beat in my chest again and a tingling feeling return in my fingers. 'He's okay?'

'I don't know. We need to go.'

She dropped me at the front door, saying she would find me after parking. I raced to the emergency department, which was over-crowded with men in bandages, moaning on stretchers lining the halls. Nurses and doctors hustled, some wrapped bandages on patients in the waiting room, others pushed crying, dirt-covered men in wheelchairs to operating rooms. I stood behind one man at reception.

'I am trying to find out more information for you, sir. I will find you as soon as I know,' the stalky brunette behind the counter said firmly.

'I've been waiting for over an hour.'

'Have a look around you.' She raised her hand to the chaotic waiting room. 'Everyone's waiting. We are at capacity. We have staff working overtime to take care of everyone. We are all trying our best. I promise you, as soon as I know more information on your son, I will let you know. I understand it must be hard, but—'

'You don't understand! It's my son!'

'Please, sir. Have a seat.'

He shook his head and walked to the vending machine in the corner of the room, punched it twice, then grabbed at his aching hand, lowered his head and cried.

The receptionist turned to me apologetically.

'It's a bit crazy in here at the moment.' Her face then lit up. 'Anna Johns?'

I closed my lips and nodded. 'I am after information on Jack McKercher. Or Jack Williams.'

'Are you a relative?'

'No, I'm—'

'Listen, we can only give out this information to relatives.'

'He doesn't have any. I'd be his next of kin. Or closest thing to.'

'Listen. No special treatment here,' she snapped and tilted her chin towards the man at the vending machine. 'Like I said to him, we are very busy.'

'I'm the only family Jack has.'

Sensing the desperation in my voice, she looked at her computer and pressed a few buttons on the keyboard. 'Jack has just come out of surgery. He's been put in Ward C, Room 34. You will have to ask the nurses on shift if you can see him.'

After a short jog through the halls and up three levels of stairs, I stopped outside his room and peered through the half-open blinds on the large internal window. He was hooked up to a ventilator, his face swollen and pale, and a bandage wrapped around the top of his ear. His bare arms were bandaged and bruised and an IV was hooked to his hand.

Though he was battered and broken, he looked at peace. A nurse walked past me and opened the door.

'Can I come in?'

'Are you family?' she asked.

'Nearly.'

She waved me inside and I sat in the chair next to his bed as she checked his charts.

'Jack is very lucky,' she said as she jotted notes. 'He was in the mine shaft when the blast occurred. He's one of the lucky ones who got pulled to safety. Took a hard fall and suffered a concussion, broken ribs and a punctured lung, which they've just operated on. He's currently in an induced coma, but he should make a full recovery.'

I sighed a breath of relief and grabbed at his hand. The sound of his steady heartbeat was like music to my ears. I looked at the bulging blue veins in his hand and pressed against them, hoping to feel the blood run through. The warmth in his hands was enough.

The nurse left the room. Mum stood in the hall, looking through the window, a half-smile drawn across her wilted face. She raised her fingers in a semi-solute, and I waved back. She held up her mobile and shook it, tucked it in her pocket and walked away.

I stayed by Jack's side for the next twenty-four hours, praying that every breath he took would bring him closer to waking. Mum stopped in the following day and brought me clothes, food and books.

Jimmy called to check how I was going. He was in Byron Bay, had a weekend gig in a small pub, and was exploring the area during the day. He said he would come back, but I told him not to and that I would be fine. Hearing him speak of his new adventure felt like a small ray of light within the four, dark and sterile hospital walls I had developed a new appreciation for. Those walls didn't just confine death, they held new beginnings too.

Lucas stopped in too. I met him in the hallway outside the room.

'How is he?'

'Not great, but he will be.'

'Like our friendship? I hope?'

'Hopefully.'

He reached into his laptop bag slung across his chest and grabbed the magazine I had bought for him. 'I wanted to return it.'

I held up my hands. 'Keep it. It was a gift.'

'I don't deserve it.'

I folded my arms across my chest.

He took a deep breath and put it back in his bag. 'I don't know how I'll repay you.'

'You can start by being the good guy you've always been. Don't sell yourself to the man to get further ahead. You can get lost in ambition. I did.'

'I can start there.' He smirked. 'Well, I should go. I just wanted to check in, and to say I'm sorry. And I'm here if you need a friend.'

'Thank you.'

After I'd spent thirty-six hours sitting helplessly next to Jack, Sam arrived to drag me out of the hospital. She walked into the room with two takeaway coffees, a sandwich from the bakery and a smirk.

'Just for half an hour,' she said.

'I can't, Sam—'

'He's not going anywhere.' She giggled inappropriately. 'If he wakes, you'll be back by the time the nurses are done with him. He knows you're here, pleading with him to wake up. He knows. He can hear you. He'd want you to take a break. And he'd really want you to have a shower.'

For the first time in days, I laughed. 'Okay. Half an hour, and a shower.'

Back at my parents' house, Sam waited with Mum downstairs while I embraced the warm, powerful flow of water pounding against my skin – my first shower since I'd left New York. I dried off, changed into fresh clothes and sat quietly with Sam and Mum, sinking my teeth into my bakery sandwich and washing it down with lukewarm coffee. Their words were a blur, my eyes heavy.

'Sit for a while on the couch, Ruby. Relax for five minutes. When you want to go back, Sam will drive you,' Mum insisted.

As soon as I laid my head on the couch, I fell into blackness. I woke to the sound of kookaburras in the dark. I checked my mobile. Not one missed call. I sat up, pushed aside the blanket Mum must have laid on me, walked to the front door and grabbed Mum's car keys off the front table.

'Ruby, it's five in the morning,' Dad called from the top of the stairs, wrapped in a blue fleece robe.

'I didn't mean to wake you.'

Each step creaked as he walked towards me. 'Go back to sleep, please. You need some rest.'

'I feel good now, Dad. I've had too much sleep. I need to get back.'

'Then let me take you.'

I reluctantly agreed. We drove in silence until he dropped me at the front entrance. Though I knew it was on his mind, Dad never once told me I shouldn't be there. He didn't tell me that I deserved better, or that I was making a mistake.

He put his hand on my back. 'He's a lucky man to have you stay by his side despite his past.'

'We all have one.' I said, and just before I closed the door, I leaned back inside. 'Thanks, Dad.'

I walked to Jack's room and peered in, expecting to see Jack how I had left him – alone and strapped to a machine. But a nurse was standing at the side of his bed, speaking with him and writing in a chart, while he stared at her, his arms still wrapped in bandages and folded on his stomach.

A PLAN UNRAVELLED

When the nurse finished asking questions, she stuck the chart next to his bed, adjusted his pillow and gave him a sip of water, which he sucked through a straw, wincing as he swallowed. He watched the nurse as she headed to the door, then noticed me staring through the blinds. I lifted my hand and gave him a small grin. I'd waited for the moment he would wake, I imagined he would beam from ear to ear and tell me he loved me, but as he stared, tired and helpless, doubts raced through my mind.

The nurse held the door open for me, and I made my way to the dreaded wicker chair. He watched as I sat next to him, then slowly lifted his arm and let out a croaky whisper. 'Come here.'

I leaned in towards his face, and coerced by his hands, pressed my lips against his. They were rough but warm. He kissed me slowly and softly for only a second. I opened my mouth and breathed in his hot air, then carefully kissed a piece of uninjured skin on his cheek and lifted my nose to his.

'Hey.' He smiled.

'Hey.'

'You came back.'

'I should have never left.'

He patted the bed. I slipped off my shoes and lay on what little space there was next to him, wrapped my arm around his stomach, careful not to put any pressure on his wounds or pull at any chords. We lay there for hours, only parting when the doctor entered.

For the next few days, I helped Jack to and from a wheelchair, because his ribs hurt too much for him to walk without a hunch. I waited next to him while he was monitored and had his bandages changed. I rubbed his shoulders and back when they ached. We watched television, we sat on the grass outside and, when it was approved, I wheeled him around the street for fresh air.

We were on one of our many walks when a passing semi-truck hit a speed bump nearby and the trailer let out a loud rattle. Jack jumped and jerked his head around.

'It's okay, it's okay.' I grabbed his face and held his stare.

He puffed his cheeks.

'Are you alright?'

'Yup.'

I pushed the wheelchair towards an empty park bench on a hospital footpath and sat next to him.

'I can't begin to imagine what that explosion was like.'

Jack's hands were interlocked as he spun his thumbs around each other. He bit his bottom lip.

'You've been through a lot,' I said.

'I was late for my shift.'

His face was scrunched like it was when he'd unleashed all his emotions at the racetrack. He had the same guilty glaze in his eyes.

'Jack, that's a good thing.'

'I should have been down there with the guys,' he whispered.

'There's a reason you weren't.'

'Just like there's a reason I didn't die years ago?'

'I don't know why things happen but...'

He buried his head in his arms.

I grabbed his head and placed it on my shoulder. 'I think you are here on this earth for a reason, Jack. Maybe it's for me. You've made me happier in these past three months than I have ever been. And when I heard that you were at work that day, I thought I might never hold you again.'

Jack straightened his back and rubbed his tears with his thumb. 'The noise was deafening, Ruby.'

I stared into his sad eyes.

'My body just flung against the cage as it plummeted. The other guys were thrown into me, our heads crashed against the wires, then I can't remember what happened. We must have been pulled out because when I came to, I was laying on the ground with men screaming around me. It felt like glass shards were stuck in my skin and a truck was on my chest. I just thought, This is it. I'm finally getting what I deserve.'

'Jack,' I pleaded. 'You have to stop punishing yourself. You've been given another chance. Don't throw it away like you did the first time. Live.'

'I should have told you.'

'Stop, Jack. I know now—'

'I should have told you to stay. And I should have told you that I love you, Ruby. Before you left for New York. I should have told you. Because I do.'

Thirty-Four

Jack began to rebuild, as did the rest of Rockford. The town mourned fourteen dead, and an investigation was launched into exactly how the explosion occurred. The government discussed closing the mine, but most locals protested the move, including the surviving miners and the families of the deceased. They wanted safer work practices for the employees, but insisted that a town built on the back of the mine would fall apart if it was closed. Hundreds protested at the mine, in front of the media circus that followed, chanting with posters painted with slogans such as MOVING FORWARD and WHEN DISASTER STRIKES, WE RISE ABOVE.

There were private funerals and public memorials. People flung their arms around each other when they met on the streets, bought grieving families their coffees or lunches, or poured out their own frustrations and drowned their sorrows over pints of beer and bottles of wine. Sam said The Night Owl was a dark place to be and she felt herself slumping into a depression, crying in Harry's arms at night. If it wasn't for him, Sam said, she would have packed her things and fled town.

Dad worked late again. This time for certain, buried under paperwork. Lucas was by his side also working long hours.

I called Michelle and told her I wasn't coming back, and that I was leaving New York for good. She fought tooth and nail against my decision, but I stayed firm. I told her to sell my apartment and take a hefty percentage of the sale.

My knotted stomach had begun to ease, I was full of energy, and I didn't know if it was the comfort of being in Jack's bed, or the fact that we were finally relaxed, that I could now sleep at night.

After some coercion, I convinced Jack to make contact with his estranged mother. Within forty-eight hours of the call, she was at his house cradling his bruised head in her bony hands and she wept.

In the evening, I sat with her in Jack's small kitchen, sipping tea and swapping stories. I spoke of my life in New York – the narrow streets, the unending skyline, the arts and culture, the busyness of it all. She shared memories of when Jack was little – the time he first learned to ride a bike. It was red with ape-hanger handlebars and Spokey Dokeys on the wheels that noisily clinked together on every rotation. He was wearing his favourite blue and white top with a picture of a yellow tractor on the front. He rode about ten metres down a dirt road when he lost control and slid down an embankment.

'His knees were scraped and small pebbles were stuck in his tiny hands. His face and hair were full of mud and grass.' She said nostalgically. 'I gave him a cuddle and told him I would get a bandage for his knee, but he was just crying because he had torn his favourite shirt.'

She spoke with such precision, as if she were flipping through an old photo album, wiping the dust from each picture's story, which she had captured in her mind. She laughed and shook her head, then sipped her tea. With a crooked nose and piercing blue eyes, she stared blankly at the wall above me – just like Jack did on his scotch-drinking nights – her thoughts stuck on a page from the past.

I grabbed the teapot and refilled both out empty cups, snapping her back to reality.

'As he got older, there were more bumps and bruises.' She brought the steaming cup to her cracked lips. Her nails were slightly yellow and the smell of cigarettes tainted her breath. 'He was always a bit of an adventurous one. He gave anything a go, Ruby. He was the first of his friends to try rollerblading, then when that got boring, he made jumps in the backyard. He eventually bought a skateboard, then moved on to wakeboarding with a few friends whose parents had boats. Then snowboarding. I don't know if he does any of that anymore?'

She looked to me for an answer. I shrugged.

'He used to have a life about him. A sparkle in his eyes. He seemed to love life until his father left.' She turned her wet eyes back to me. 'You think you know someone.'

'I'm sorry.' I whispered.

'I worked three jobs to make ends meet, and I struggled. Jack knew it. If I'd known what he was doing to keep us from getting snowed under in bills, to help put food on the table, I would have made him stop. I would have. But I didn't know. I was never home, so how could I? And if he'd known that his best friend and girlfriend would die as a consequence, he wouldn't have done it either. When he was locked up, I blamed myself.

'I should have been there when he got out. But I couldn't face him. And I didn't think he could face me. I'd failed him. When I got the call that my ex-husband's mother had died and left the house to her only grandson, I thought, This is it. He can start fresh. Without me. I left our house while he packed and we didn't even say goodbye.

'I wondered every day if Jack was okay. Every. Day.'

We sat in silence for a few minutes, listening to the ticking of the clock and sipping the remainder of our tea.

When the tea ran out, our conversation did too.

'You take care of my boy, okay?'

After three nights of sleeping on the couch in Jack's house, she packed her bags and this time, said goodbye. She told Jack that she would be back as soon as work would allow, if he wanted her to.

I didn't tell Jack about the conversation I'd had with his mother. I assumed it was the first time she'd spoken about the incident, releasing the guilt she had carried for years. I only hoped that Jack had done the same.

Thirty-Five

May, One Year Later.

'Please, everyone. Take your seats. The show is about to begin.' Jimmy stood behind the microphone in the backstage music control room. Headphones smothered his tiny ears, and the whites of his eyes glistened as he focused on the sound system in front of him.

Jack elbowed me. 'Nervous?'

'Jack, c'mon. I'm a professional.'

'But you're usually onstage, not behind the scenes.'

'I feel more comfortable here.'

He squeezed my hand. 'Good.'

I squeezed back, then clapped my hands and shouted to the cast. 'Okay, places please. Let's do this.'

Everyone scurried about, the lights went dim and the curtains opened.

Jack and I left backstage and walked into the dark seating area. The old building Jack and I had transformed into a theatre could fit about two hundred people. It was at capacity.

We quietly took our seats in the front row, next to Mum and Dad.

'He's asleep,' Mum said, passing me Leo. 'Perfect timing.'

I cradled Leo in my arms. He looked incredibly serene in his grey beanie and wrapped in a blue blanket. I brushed my finger along his smooth, chubby cheek. 'He takes after his dad,' I whispered to Jack. 'Not a huge fan of theatre.'

Jack flashed me his cheeky grin. 'He'll grow to love it. You'll make sure of it.'

'He better,' I said. 'He gave me weeks of morning sickness and sleepless nights. He owes me.'

Leo barely stirred as the script I wrote played out onstage. He didn't seem to notice when the roaring laughter filled the air or when the music Jimmy produced sounded over the speakers.

I, on the other hand, took it all in. The giggles, the snorts, the gasps, the silence.

Mum put her hand on my knee near the end of the last scene and whispered in my ears. 'Stop tapping your toes. There's nothing to worry about.'

I took a deep breath as the curtains closed and the lights went out. Applause.

When the lights came back on, I was the only person still in my seat. Jack looked down to me and winked. Mum clapped enthusiastically. Dad leaned across her.

'Go you good thing,' he said with a closed fist. 'Anna for the win.'

I nodded slowly as a single tear dropped down my cheek.

The cast came back on stage, joined hands and bowed. Jimmy followed closely behind. He pointed his hand toward me and smiled. 'Ladies and gentlemen. Anna Johns.'

ACKNOWLEDGEMENTS

Wow. What an amazing ride this experience has been. From jotting down a story idea while my firstborn napped, to having it published five years later. This book would have never been possible without the boundless support of a bunch of brilliant people.

To Elizabeth and Daniel who read *A Plan Unravelled*, believed in it and ultimately made my publishing dreams come true. I will never be able to thank you enough.

To Antoinette Holm from Writer's Victoria for your thorough assessment and guidance, and to editor extraordinaire AJ Collins for your valued input and professional advice. AJ, you not only helped fine-tune my manuscript, but also gave me the confidence to pursue and persist.

To my amazing girlfriends for your friendship, advice and encouragement. How lucky am I to have you all in my life!?

To the Spencers. Thank you for making me feel like one of your own and supporting me in all I do. I'm forever grateful.

Mum, Dad, Kelly and Michaela. You have always been my greatest supporters in everything I do. I know that the crippling fear of failing would have stopped me from chasing my dreams if it wasn't for your continued encouragement. From listening to my improvised bedtime nurseries, to keeping containers full of my unfinished stories, to bragging about my published works – you've always been my biggest fans. Thank you for believing in me.

To Jill and Aryn. You've taught me to never take for granted the people you love and that life is short, so live it to the fullest. I miss you incredibly.

To my children. Isla and Louis. Thank you for your hugs, kisses and everything in between. I'm blessed to be your mummy.

Lastly, to Michael. Thank you for your support, encouragement and your unconditional love. You're my happily ever after ;)   I'll love you, always.

CPSIA information can be obtained
at www.ICGtesting.com
Printed in the USA
LVHW040048020819
626222LV00005B/9/P

9 780648 490319